THE MISSING
WITHERTON
FILES

1962-THE CUBAN MISSILE CRISIS

MOLLY CHANDLER

WESTBOW
PRESS®
A DIVISION OF THOMAS NELSON
& ZONDERVAN

This is a work of fiction. All of the characters,
names, incidents, organizations, and dialogue in
this novel are either the products of the author's
imagination or are used fictitiously.

WestBow Press books may be ordered through
booksellers or by contacting:

WestBow Press
A Division of Thomas Nelson & Zondervan
1663 Liberty Drive
Bloomington, IN 47403
www.westbowpress.com
844-714-3454

Scripture taken from the New King James Version®. Copyright ©
1982 by Thomas Nelson. Used by permission. All rights reserved.

ISBN: 978-1-6642-0180-4 (sc)
ISBN: 978-1-6642-0163-7 (e)

Print information available on the last page.

WestBow Press rev. date: 09/23/2020

To our President, His Staff, Nation's Leaders,
And
Our beloved Military who strive to
Keep our Country Safe and Secure.
May God Keep Us Strong and Vigilant.

PROLOGUE

The year is 1962. It would be tragic for the United States Government to doze while a possible annihilation attempt could be brewing right smack at its back door.

The May afternoon had been blessed with a sunlit sky. President Kennedy stopped to peer out the window of his Oval Office- to take a breather from his steady pace of going through budget proposals. As he rubbed his chin and stretched, he heard a buzz from his desk. Attending to the phone signal, he heard his secretary say, "Sir, there's someone with news from Intel to see you, and he states it's urgent."

"Yes, send him in, Rene'. I'm free at the moment."

"Yes, Sir"

As the door opened, in walked the Presidential Advisor.

"Sir, sorry to interrupt you, but I don't need to delay this report from our Intelligence Community. It seems we have some unusual footage for you to see from our U-2 planes near the border... of-Cuba. I was told that it appears Cuba is building a nuclear arsenal right under our nose. There are amazing graphic photos gathered and sent to the Pentagon.

Word is- that there is little doubt that Cuba and Russia are conniving in a joint effort to promote a problem to the U.S. security as never before. I'm sure you will be interested in viewing all this new footage."

"Well, just hold it right there, Bundy, and let's go have a look at these. Get the staff together, and let's not waste a minute to view this footage." The President was staunch to arise from his desk, his face taut. "This seems a daring move," he stated.

As the White House was in a spiral to get to the bottom of this event, the leaders of the Defense team were preparing to discuss strategy. Word had been swiftly communicated through-out the walls of the White House and transmitted to appropriate contacts. The Pentagon would soon take steps to alert various areas of the military. If the President gave orders to alert the Armed Forces, there would be no delay in preparations.

During the on-going Presidential meetings, a member of the U.S. Department of Defense over-heard some of the military staff speaking in their closed sessions that, "word is out-that there are Russian agents in the vicinity trying to gain possession of some classified files from the U.S. Department of Defense."

Sgt. Foley was privy to the recent classified files, and he was determined they didn't-- 'land in the wrong hands.' He, discreetly, made plans to be sure the Witherton Files were not compromised. He met with Lt. Caleb Brown, another employee of the Defense Department, and they conspired to be sure these files would be transported to another locale until the present area was established as a secure crime-free zone. General Faust had already demanded an up-grade to all stored files.

After Lt. Brown gains possession of the classified files from Sgt. Foley, he interacts with Julie Peterson, a trusted former employee of the U.S. Department of Defense. She is to help him further secure the files. Ms. Peterson agrees to the meet Lt. Caleb Brown for the clandestine transfer of the Witherton Files back to a more secure area with General Faust.

While Ms. Peterson is trying to return to Topeka, Kansas, from Lt. Caleb's distant office, she is somehow detained.

Meanwhile, Julie's dear friend, Kevin Seals' mission with Special Ops is interrupted when he is involved in a plane crash. Could the two incidents be inter-related? Two missions in chaos?

Can Jay, Julie's co-worker, help unravel the mystery? Jay receives a call from Julie at the Blitz Coffee Shop in Topeka, Kansas. "The traffic and weather are horrendous, but I shall meet you soon, Jay. We have several items to discuss regarding our new assignment with the Herald." The phone then was silent...

CHAPTER
ONE

MONTEGO HOTEL, TOPEKA, KANSAS, 1962

Giving little thought to the robin's chirping or the geese squawking overhead, Jay Falk rushed head-on through the bustling streets of Topeka, Kansas. Crinkling his forehead, he tried to deny his recent anxiety regarding his dear friend and fellow reporter, Julie Peterson. As his heart pounded and perspiration covered his forehead, he vowed to reach her very soon. She could either call or send me word. *What's up, Julie? This is not your style: to keep me in the dark. She should be here! We've a job to do, and I'm not giving in to her hesitations.*

Spotting the coffee shop up ahead, Jay fast paced in that direction. He needed patience, patience. He knew he should get a call soon and this fretting would turn into unnecessary worry. I mustn't allow Julie to question my surfing; that's not an option. The Western Herald had confirmation the Witherton Files were missing: and, the U.S. Defense Department needed answers.

Being a senior reporter with the Iowa Herald didn't help Jay in Topeka. He was contemplating a great story once he and Julie located the missing Witherton Files for the Western Herald. *We need to be moving in that direction.*

A steady breeze began to whip across his face as Jay approached the third street west of Princeton Boulevard. He tripped on a broken stone and almost went down. Muscles tightened as he straightened his stance. He needed two or three mugs of strong coffee with Julie close by: that would help his dilemma, he was positive. He kicked the broken pebbles along the street in sudden frustration.

Noting a chill from the spring breeze which stirred the leaves of the budding oaks nearby, he snuggly embraced his gray wool coat. Even with his layered mauve shirt and pin-stripe tie, he could still feel a dampness in the air. Could be a weather change, Jay noted, as he turned his gaze toward the Western sky.

A left turn, and none too soon, Jay reached The Blitz Coffee Shoppe. Grasping the brass door handle, he hurried inside to face- none other than- Bill Finlay, an overstuffed employee of the Western Herald, sitting directly in front of him with a wide grin on his face.

"Hey, Jay, I've been waiting for you to come in. I knew you were back in town from Julie's conversations. She sure is a looker. Is she coming by; or, you keeping her to yourself?" Bill arose and met Jay with a handshake. Motioning him to his table, Bill waved his hand for Jay to sit at an angle from him and beckoned the waitress to accommodate him. No sooner had they shaken hands, than Bill immediately started his query. "Say, did you know that Julie Peterson got the Witherton File assignment?"

Jay's eyebrows raised. Stunned was not the word. He ignored Bill's comment stating, "I'm aware of some communication, but not details. I plan to meet-up with her today to discuss various work projects. What other information do you have, Bill? Am I out of the loop again?"

"Oh, tidbits here, and there. Are you in this with her, Jay, or meeting her on other ties?" He chuckled.

Jay let Bill's comment slide. "She's sure to call me soon." Surely, the Herald didn't release this info to Bill. He don't realize how confidential this assignment is, or he'd not spout off.

Peering out the window, he sought to divert Bill's query. "You know Julie is a seasoned reporter and investigator. She'll be well informed on her projects. I only hope my investigative skills can match hers. I'm just returning to the Herald to begin anew, Bill." He gazed back at the guy who chose to spout off. He could imagine Julie's large hazel eyes glaring back at Bill as she tossed her lustrous brown hair to the side to reveal her smooth olive skin, and sculpted· neckline. She'd shield her glare in an attempt to mask her outrage at Bill's comments.

Jay had worked with Julie before and he knew she could fulfill her callings. "Bill, her skills and flexibility are commendable; that's how she gets top assignments." Jay dared not mention her other assets, like wonderful physique and grace with each step she took. *Keep him guessing, that's my plan.*

Jay's cell phone vibrated to interrupt his focus. "Excuse me, Bill." Taking the call from Julie, he noted her urgency as she spoke of heavy rainfall impeding her progress. Speaking gently, he assured her that he would see her as soon as she arrived. He urged her to please take caution and drive with care. After his counsel, he bade her goodbye and silenced his phone.

Both men were silent as Jay finished his latte. He, then, arose from his seat and faced Bill with a stare. "Bill, you amaze me with your knowledge, but my duty calls." He turned to leave, afraid he might call Bill's hand if he spoke again.

Bill called out, "It's great to hear from Julie. I'm glad she's safe. Keep me posted, Jay. I'm kind of amazed at why this is such an assignment that it takes two to collect information."

"Well, this is America, Bill. Free enterprise."

Leaving the Blitz, Jay entered the driver's seat of his 1962 silver SUV, and headed back to his hotel. He still cringed to remember Bill's bold remarks. His gab was not welcome from someone who usually had no interest in his or Julie's goings-on at the Herald. *I'll not dwell upon Bill, but I don't wish leaks of important information either.*

◄►

Approaching the Montego Hotel, Jay noted the animal clinic where his shepherd dog, Jojo was boarding. The clinic was nestled among auto shops and other equipment and hardware stores. He stopped to notify Payne that his dog would need to stay a few more days. "Payne, I'm on assignment again, and Jojo needs to stay here a few more days. Can you keep an eye on him? I need my full attention on my work these days."

"Sure, Jay. He's a fine shep, and I have plenty of space. No problem. How's the Herald coming? I really enjoy the paper. You just keep the good news coming. Maybe not so much bad," He chuckled.

"We're good. We have some great up-coming stories. Just keep updated. Good to see you attending to my buddy here." Jay kept patting Jojo... "Just hating to leave... He turned and waved goodbye as he exited the clinic and returned to his vehicle. He stroked his chin, and stirred the car toward the Montego Hotel.

Jay remembered how his dog had rescued him many times when he worked with Chief Jarod. Jojo had a keen sense of obedience and always kept a watchful eye when on duty. He failed to mention to Payne that he was a K-9 dog worth more than money could buy. "I hope he's pampered daily at the kennel, like he is at home," he sighed.

Hurrying on to his hotel, he entered his room to slip into his beige, oversized cushioned recliner. Pulling off his tie, he stretched. Massaging his head, he scoured his brain to ponder Finlay's remarks and interest in his and Julie's assignment. He raised his head upright as he recalled Bill's role, "Yes! I do know, he's affiliated with research and data collection with international connections (whatever that involves, maybe traffic too, for all

I know," he muttered. *I can't wait to get Julie's take on all of this gab.*

Jay tried to reach Julie by phone for the third attempt. But, he only reached a busy signal. Must be in heavy traffic, or otherwise detained, he gathered as he closed his phone.

Leaning back in his cozy recliner, he could hear the sound of rain drops-pitter patter-on the window pane. He sat there and began to nod his head in sleep as the rhythmic drops coaxed him into... another time.

Julie knew her rendezvous wasn't without danger as she chose to meet Lieutenant Caleb Brown. He had called saying, "meet me at a secluded cabin in the hills near Sandy Mountain. I need you to deliver some classified files for me from this location, twenty miles north-west of Topeka, Kansas." She trusted him, although unsure of the rational. Was it her good fortune to get these without specifics? She must be diligent.

Approaching the cabin, she hurried to the rustic door and gently knocked. Her body was beginning to shake as she waited.

When Lieutenant Caleb opened the door, he nodded and peered both ways before he invited her in. "My the clouds are gathering outside, and the wind is picking up. Hope we're not in for more stormy weather," he mentioned as he closed the door.

"I've been expecting you, Julie. Good to see you again. I knew I could depend on you. Glad you could transfer these files to be secured for us on such short notice." He smiled and offered her a cushioned chair near his desk. "Coffee?" he asked.

"Ye..s," she trembled. "Lieutenant Caleb, I'm trying to get back to Topeka before the weather worsens." She shivered. *Am I afraid?* She clung to her cup, her hands trembling.

"Julie, I received these files from an officer and friend. I know of your concern, but my cohort overheard someone in the Service speaking of how the Russians were looking for certain classified files in our department. They talked about their own resources confiscating them for their benefit. It can't happen! My officer friend thought these files needed more security for our government at this crucial time."

"Julie, take these, and do not let them land in the wrong hands. It could jeopardize the lives of many."

"Thanks, Lieutenant, I'll expedite the delivery process as soon as possible. I must be going before more clouds gather or flash floods develop." Gazing around the room, her eyes surveyed every inch and cranny of the office space. After his further instructions, she arose and shook Caleb's hand, then exited with the Files. She still failed to understand how the officer obtained the files, or how the Russians gained their knowledge. But, Caleb trusted her. Now, she had the ball... to get rolling.

◄◄

When Julie departed Caleb's office, the Lieutenant speed called General Seth Faust of the U.S. Defense Department. "General, I have released the Witherton Files to Julie Peterson. Remember her? She should see the files safely delivered to a secure area of the U.S. Defense Department. She's reliable."

"Sir, I came upon these files from Officer Jim Foley. You recall the story of his from our previous conversation. He was using our best interest to protect the files. General, allow me to place you on hold while I attend to a matter."

Lieutenant Brown's eyebrows were raised at the appearance of Officer Foley at his door. The six-foot, six-inch newcomer to the Defense Department had entered. With his dreary, slanted eyes, and slumped shoulders, he straightened and saluted.

"Where is the leak of info, Officer Foley?" Caleb asked, as he motioned him to be seated. Lt. Caleb contemplated Foley's prior visit, but saw little need to remind him again.

Foley raised his shoulders. "Who knows, Sir? I came as soon as I gathered the files yesterday and deposited them into your capable hands. I was trying to be ensure their utmost security."

"I've been too busy for this new development, Sgt. Foley. But, we'll deal with it, and I'll see that this gets the proper attention needed. Just keep this quiet, will you? Don't think I'll fail and buckle under the Kremlin's tactics, even with this threat of a breach in the security of our files!"

"My lips are sealed, Sir. I don't wish to create more static than has already been stirred." Foley confessed.

"I have a friend who did work with General Faust at the U.S. Department of Defense who still has security clearance, and she is capable of restoring the classified files to the area of maximum security. How they've been targeted in the beginning is a mystery to me. Excuse me, Officer Foley, I need to see to this matter pronto." Caleb showed Foley the door, and he exited.

Lt. Caleb resumed the phone call. "General, as I was sa...

"Lieutenant Brown, this seems a clandestine manner to secure the files. But, if you are sure of their safe delivery, what can I say? I'm depending on you, our nation is in peril, Lieutenant."

"Thanks, General, I shall personally see that the classified files are back in your possession and you can see to their safe disposition again. Ms. Peterson is now working with the Western Herald, but she should get the files to you soon, General. Once you've upgraded your records department, any additional threats should be diminished. Any problems, just contact me at my office tomorrow. I should be back into the area by noon. I'll promptly call as soon as I return to the U.S. Defense Department. I still have a few unanswered questions for you; I'll run those by to get your input, Sir. Have a nice day, General."

Julie sped along Highway I-20 en route to the Western Herald, and the Montego Hotel. Although she had left the Sandy Mountain cabin with intent to meet Jay Falk on time, the rain was already hindering her progress. As rain pelted on her windshield, she had to slow her speed. Julie had assured her coworker that she would see him by eleven a.m. at the Montego Hotel, but the traffic was horrendous.

Why, oh why, can't I get a grip on this wheel, she wondered as a downpour was evident. If this weather improves, I can reach my destination on time. Her mind began to remember leaving Kevin's tender embrace and warmth prior to departing from his home last evening. Her fond memories brought a smile to her face. She hoped he was well on his way to Aguadilla, Puerto Rico, for his military assignment.

She and Kevin had been very close since she had met him two years ago while on assignment. Her duty then was to head-up a leading story of pilots in defense training for special-ops missions at his base. Kevin had raised eyebrows then, and now, with his expertise in flight and mission accomplishments. His strong dedication to his country could not be overlooked. His safety was always her primary concern, especially, since she had heard news of Russian involvement with our neighbor, the Cuban government. *We could not turn our heads at this news.*

Moving ahead of heavy traffic, she recalled her objective. She and Jay Falk were to make a report of locating the classified military files in her possession: she had been forthcoming to use her previous contacts to obtain these. They were to forward these files to the U.S. Defense Department personnel: safely out of enemy hands. She had not yet confided in Jay.

Julie was about to turn on to the Lakewood exit, when she noticed a black Mercedes sedan getting much too close to her vehicle. She surely hoped this was not someone trying some foul play in this deluge of rain. This was not a time for things to go wrong. She must protect the files regardless of the cost. If Jay had come with me, I would not be so uneasy. He would know how to protect me.

Julie heard the screeching of tires behind her as she signaled to turn right at her exit. *He's too close! What's the idea with him?* Thru her rearview mirror she could barely make out what looked like a blond-haired guy- intent upon her. He could spell trouble. *He could be aware of the files I carry. I should have hidden the Witherton Files underneath my seat compartment- out of sight! What was I thinking? If I can get away from this dude, I'll pull over and hide the files.* She grasped the wheel tighter as perspiration covered her forehead. Her body was rigid. *He's almost on my bumper.*

She sped up her vehicle, but he immediately increased his speed. Glancing into her rearview mirror again... *Oh, my, help. I'm hit...*

THREE

Kevin Lee Seals, to his friends, was a striking young pilot with blonde hair and piercing blue eyes, whose confidence made him a commanding presence. He had a distinct love for flying that superseded most young recruits in his group of trainees. He loved to soar into the heavens with his comrades in the U.S. Air Force.

Sergeant Percales smiled and commented to him after observing his flight maneuvers. "You're one of our elite pilots, Lieutenant Seals. And, we believe in your abilities to conquer the skies"!

Seals smiled, "Thank you, Sir." Having just returned from a practice drill at Aguadilla, Puerto Rico, the threesome, Nettles, Seals, and Percales had flown close maneuvers for the last few weeks. They were excelling in speed and performance.

"I've already told him as much, Sir," his good friend, Sergeant Nettles replied knowingly. "Julie's aware also." Kevin's wide grin spoke what his words failed to utter. *Who's been reading my mind?* He almost broke his silence. He could certainly recall his visits with Julie while on leave. But he wasn't going to elaborate on his personal life at the moment.

After Kevin had completed his series of preparation flights, and gained security clearance from his Command Center, he was summoned to report to Colonel O'Neal the next day promptly at eight a.m. *I'm unsure of this meeting, and why I'm told to report to the Colonel: I hope there's no change in my assignment.*

Having a restless night, when morning came, Kevin hurriedly dressed, anxious to get on with the meeting.

Arriving early at the Colonel's plush office: all leather furniture, large walnut desk, almond-textured walls, tailored, floor to ceiling, mauve-to cranberry drapes (the works): *not like our quarters,* he was quick to observe. Kevin entered, saluted, and was greeted by his superior with a warm smile and handshake.

"Good to see you in great shape again. I have some good news for you." Colonel O'Neal was forthcoming.

Thoughtful, Kevin dared to question. "What is it, Sir? Am I going to get a special leave, or is this something else?"

"Well, just give me a minute: I'll explain with details. Lieutenant Seals, first of all, I'm very pleased with your practice runs and training exercises. It seems you've come a long way since first arriving at Ramey Air Base. And, you may realize the U. S. is undergoing some unusual and serious entanglements with other countries."

"Is this in regard to Cuba? Are we facing a crisis?"

"Absolutely, we are on alert, Kevin."

"Anything that I can help with, you know that I am willing, Sir."

"You know that is exactly what I like to hear, Lieutenant. And, I do have a mission for you starting tomorrow. I know this is a little premature, but this delivery we're planning needs to get underway without delay. I shall give you a call at six p.m. today to meet me at a specific area. Don't be late."

"Yes, Sir, I'll be expecting your call."

"You shall be briefed on every aspect of the event, Kevin. And, I'm depending on you to see this through."

"Yes, Sir, See you then" Kevin replied. He stood, saluted, and turned to leave.

Leaving the Colonel's office, his spirits were high... still, the Lieutenant was mystified over the urgent developments.

I must surely get in touch with Julie. I hope she will be aware of the crisis, and my need to proceed. If I had known sooner, I could have given her a head's up and prepared her and mom, days ago. Rubbing his head, he headed out for his living quarters. He had to gather all his gear and be ready for instructions this evening. Tomorrow would be upon him, before he could get a few winks of shut-eye...

Saluting Colonel O'Neal promptly at six p.m. in a consultant suite near the Colonel's office, Kevin approached his desk noting O'Neal's demeanor: focused, not a hint of hesitancy upon his squared shoulders.

"Hello, Lieutenant," the Colonel wasted little time.

"As I said earlier, I have your first assignment planned to the letter. You know I'm depending upon you to get this mission up and running. Like I said, our country is in dire circumstances, and we need to proceed with fervor, and precision."

"You are our best prepared officer for this flight, Lieutenant. You are to depart this base tomorrow, and deliver cargo containing a sophisticated warhead to Elgin Air Base in U. S. It is to be a pattern for other developments circulated around the globe, as the need arises. You were cleared through security: this is a definite confidential situation. Those involved are only aware on a 'need to know' basis. Do you understand?"

"Most, definite, Sir. I'm willing to follow this service through for my country."

"Your transport plane will be well-equipped and loaded. You should be at the hangar early, and ready for a successful flight with take-off by early morning, seven o'clock to be exact. There shall be a refueling plane scheduled to meet you in the Caribbean. C.J. shall have your flight pattern and can pin point your location as needed."

"Thanks, Sir." Shaking his superior's hand, he saluted and gathered his documents to leave. "See you as soon as I return, Sir." He smiled and departed the room.

Back in his bunker, Seals quietly reviewed his plans and the documents he was to deliver to the Commander at the Elgin Air Base. When he was satisfied with his review, his thoughts went back to Julie.

She sure seemed upset when I called about my early mission. Wish I could have prepared her sooner. Maybe I'll return before she has time to worry.

◀◀

Bright rays of sunshine greeted him the next morning as he arrived at the hangar. "Hello Lieutenant, I see you're ready to meet the skies," the overly enthused C-120 attendant halted as he was speaking to Officer Kevin. "Hope you have a splendid flight, and see you back here soon, Sir."

"Yes, yes. On to the blue yonder," Kevin replied. "But, first allow me to check all my gear and cargo thoroughly to reorient myself on my preparedness... Everything looks in place, and I hear the weather should be great."

"That's correct, Lieutenant. Most beautiful spring day, for your flight. Any problems, the control tower should address them promptly. Stay focused, and all should be well with you."

After Kevin satisfied himself with his preparations, he strapped himself into his seat and was at the controls. Within minutes he was reaching the skies with a steady takeoff.

Several hours later he was nearing the Caribbean. As night began to approach, he noticed a stream of fog. There had been little turbulence. *I should be reaching my refueling plane soon. I'm making good progress.*

Trying to update his weather awareness, Kevin noted his fuel gauge was a little lower than noted earlier. I need to locate C.J .real soon...

CHAPTER
FOUR

Kevin had known there could be trouble when he encountered a dense fog while trying to reach his refueling plane. Being over the Caribbean, he had hoped to just refuel, and be on his way to his destination near the Gulf Coast at Elgin Air Base. He would then store his warhead and reroute back to Puerto Rico: a simple task.

"Heaven help," he uttered as he noted his fuel was almost gone. He was already beginning to lose altitude. "What the ... Sam Hill?.. "Mayday, mayday, mayday," Kevin radioed for help. Perspiring, and tense, he cabled the tower with his distress call. "I'm going down... my refueling plane is nowhere to be found."

As Kevin began his descent toward the Caribbean waters, he knew he had no choice but to eject from his aircraft. He quickly grabbed his life jacket and gear with parachute. His heart was running in overtime mode. Not a minute to spare, he prepared for emergency survival. Hoping to reach help, he called the tower again. He heard someone bellow out, "do what you must, we'll send out a rescue crew."

As the plane sputtered in descent, Kevin grasped

his ejection device with precision. With parachute in tow, he descended to battle the ocean.

Landing in the cool waters of the ocean, Kevin feared for his life. There wasn't a raft anywhere to be seen. "I'll surely die," he uttered as he watched his plane plummet a long distance from where he went down.

Calling upon God for protection, Kevin strived to stay afloat with his gear attached to him. Managing to get rid of his parachute, he realized he still had three flares he could use in his waterproof gear. If he could spot a vessel or plane, he might get help. Shivering, he watched the sun setting in the western sky. His hope was for more warmth, as his body cried out from the nights oncoming chill. As darkness engulfed him, he failed to relax enough to blink an eye... *Just keep afloat and keep watch... if only he could hear a motor.*

As the sun crested the next morning, he tried to move his body more to gain extra strength- to little avail. Just to stay afloat, and keep his eyes and ears alert for sight or sound of any approaching traffic, that was a tiresome effort. Praying to God for deliverance was his only hope. *His faith was being challenged.*

Kevin was trying to sort-out his location with his equipment, when he suddenly dropped part of his gear. *Ouch* .

In the water two days was not good. Hot in the daytime and cold at night, he cried out as his muscles ached with pain.

Watching the sunrise, in his dreary state, he had been in his basic location three days with only sips of water from his canteen and bites of trail mix for survival. Having dropped part of his gear, he was dazed. He heard a roar. *Is it a dream or real?* He reached inside his gear and managed to grasp a flare. He tossed it into the air with all his strength. The plane was coming closer, a seaplane... He would be rescued.

The seaplane hovered closer and came to a halt near Kevin. A small raft was released, and two men came near. One bearded looking guy assisted him into the raft... he· would be safe.

As he was soon hoisted into the seaplane, the two men jumped back into the plane, and the rescuers sped off for Cuba with the American aboard. The rescuers were assured per radio as they called the Cuban militia, that the survivor would be fully interrogated: their-prize-catch-of-the day.

-◄◄

The two rescuers grinned and chatted with enthusiasm at their good fortune to capture an American. Speaking of further recognition, they landed near Cuban shores. Not attentive to any d1scomfort their prisoner suffered, they rode the waves to deposit the American. When they reached shore, they hefted Kevin onto a stretcher. He'd be transported to the militia. As the Cubans departed the shore in answer to another Coast Guard summons, their adrenalin was pumped-up to top speed with excitement. "Who would have believed we could salvage a lieutenant in these waters? He was in Cuban territory, ·you know, Cortez. I can assure you our

Coast Guard will be pleased with our find." Senior Gomez threw his hat in the ocean with glee. He had been privileged to learn the English language from his Spanish-American mom. She had taught him and Cortez at an early age. They enjoyed jiving with each other in English, "jest for practice,' they exclaimed. They flaunted their knowledge to elevate their moods on good or bad days at sea.

"What we need is a fiesta," Cortez whipped-up the excitement: shaking his hands in the air and rotating his hips, he sang, 'hail to Fidel, who wishes us well.' "We'll have us a roll-out tonight with our friends at the Casablanca Plaza, brother. 'Whoopee,'" he shouted.

As they were nearing their summoned call, they could scarcely contain themselves. If Cortez had known they would need to celebrate, he could have grabbed his guitar earlier.

Time is lapsing; it's almost noon, Jay sighed.

He tried to reach Julie by phone, but only reached her voice mail. He knew she was coming from I-20 to Lakewood; that was the best route. Tired of waiting, Jay decided maybe he could just meet her, or discover her whereabouts. He hesitated to notify the authorities of her absence. No one at the Herald seemed unduly concerned. After all she was on assignment; he was the one keeping tabs on her since she was his partner in the assignment.

Jay had driven a few miles along I-20 without seeing any sign of Julie's car. He was about to exit onto Lakewood, when he saw what appeared to be skid marks along the highway. Following along the Lakewood Road, he thought he might need to survey the area as he drove. About a mile from the exit he noticed more skid marks. 'I'll just pull off to investigate, he uttered. Stepping out of the car, he began to follow the tire tracks to spot a nearby ravine.

As his gaze followed the tracks, he saw a vehicle. Near the side-window someone slumped over the steering wheel. His breathing increased as he flipped his phone to call an ambulance; hurrying to assist the victim, he could hardly dial 911.

He reached the car as the ambulance suddenly arrived on the scene. *It is Julie and she appears unconscious.* He struggled to catch his breath.

Jay silenced his phone after speaking with the dispatcher; *Someone has already called 911! Thankfully, they're here.* He waited to hear her status from the paramedics as he tried to assist them to get her from the car.

━◄◄

Drake the ambulance attendant accessed Julie. "Yes, the victim is unconscious, but her vitals are okay,"

"O', I just knew something had happened! Julie is usually prompt to her appointments," Jay cried. He reached to feel her forehead and saw blood from a wound, but the ambulance attendant placed a combine dressing with pressure on the wound. This halted the blood flow. They, then, lifted her to the stretcher.

Jay scoured her vehicle, and noted her purse and briefcase were still in her car, "I'm Julie's business associate, Drake. I've been searching for her since she called me earlier en route to Topeka. I was uneasy about her location; and, that's when I located her car down this scrubby ravine. Please get her help. I can secure her belongings until her family arrives."

Jay noted her mom's phone number in Julie's billfold and was prompt to call her about the accident, He, then headed out to assist as needed. His hands trembled as he struggled to climb the muddy embankment with her belongings. He stumbled to the top.

Reaching the road, the ambulance driver was quick to secure the stretcher into the ambulance. With his attendants, he sped off to the West-End Hospital with Jay in pursuit in his SUV.

Evaluating Julie in the ER, the doctor revealed to Jay, "we'll treat her wound, and then, she'll be placed in ICU. Her condition is guarded. Let me know when her mom arrives, will you?"

"Sure, Doc." Jay thanked the doc, then, headed to the lobby.

While Jay awaited Cecilia in the lobby at West-End, he perused Julie's briefcase. Noticing some classified files, he promptly took Julie's files to his SUV, locking them in the trunk of the vehicle. He, then, proceeded back to the ICU unit to await Cecilia's arrival, and check on Julie. Finding her color pale and her lips crusty, he soon learned she remained unconscious, her brown-hair mussed.

Dr. Joe Payne, the neurologist had stated they could not predict when she would arouse, but they'd support her in every way possible with I.V. fluids, monitor, oxygen, etc.

Jay prayed, *Lord, watch over my friend. Strengthen,*

and restore her to good health. Protect her and her family.

Jay, next, notified the Western Herald that Julie had been located, and had been in an accident. "She is unable to answer questions at this time; not fully alert. Condition is guarded." He, then, silenced his phone as he saw Julie's mom enter the room. I *must strive not to upset her mom*, Jay kept reminding himself.

◄━

"Julie, I'm here, Look at me! Tell me what happened."

"Cecilia, I can assure you that she has not responded to us yet," Jay spoke calmly and softly, as he tried to comfort her mom. "Her car was found down a ravine. She apparently struck her head against the car window during the plunge, or the impact against a tree. Regardless, it was an effort to climb the muddy hillside to get her out of the mucky ravine. Who knows how the accident happened. I plan to definitely find out.

"I'm holding some of the files that were found in her car. But, I'll promptly return her purse and any belongings for you to hold for Julie. I must go now for personal reasons, Cecilia. Please call me if Julie regains consciousness. She must have a concussion, but her vital signs are...good. The doctor says she'll be closely monitored.

"Cecilia, she and I are working on a special assignment with the Herald. I need her input as soon as possible. Call me immediately if she arouses.

I'm not just her work associate, Cecilia, I'm her friend and confidant. I care very much for Julie; we're a team."

Jay quietly left the hospital. Back on I-20 in route to the Montego Hotel, he hoped to scrutinize Julie's files, and determine if they were the classified ones that the U.S. Defense Department were searching for.

Back at his hotel, Jay began to peruse the classified files noting the mention of a plane that was en route to Elgin Air Base with one of the U.S.'s most sophisticated warheads. This missile part was to be used as a design for future production by the Air Force. Jay called Elgin, but the plane was overdue; it should have arrived yesterday.

Deep in thought, he questioned, *could the plane have experienced problems, or crashed?* He had noticed on T.V. yesterday a newsbreak: the anchor mentioned a plane crash in the Caribbean. *Could it be Kevin's plane? If this was Kevin's plane, could his and Julie's calamities be coincidental? I must be imagining things. Maybe I'm too tired to think straight.* Flipping his phone, Jay began to dial-up to speak with a few traffic-controllers.

"Yes, Mr. Falk, there was a C-120 descent yesterday, and 'Mayday, Mayday' signals were heard several times prior to our last contact. The plane disappeared over the Caribbean. We're not sure of the pilot, or the landing." The controller was accommodating to Jay's query.

Silencing his phone, Jay flexed his muscles. *Who can render me more information on the plane or Kevin? Which base did he depart from when he began his flight?*

Jay kept scanning Julie's files for answers. He sure needed her help to get all needed information before returning the files to the U.S. Defense Department. "Why were the files taken, and why were they given to Julie in the first place?" Jay's uttered curiosity was ballooning, and he sighed with speculation.

Is Julie being setup to be captured? The Russians...They sure would enjoy information on the U.S. military capabilities. I need some answers. I remember a report I heard on the Today News that the Cuban Crisis was now gaining momentum, and that the President was calling upon the U.N. to try to halt the Soviet missile build- up in Cuba. Time is crucial. I must find some answers. If Julie is in over her head before I could help her to report, I need to know about it and squelch it immediately. Jay kept speculating, and trying to sort out the possibilities for events taking place.

CHAPTER
SIX

"Um-Oh-where am I?" Julie groaned.

"Julie, are you awake?" Her mom had just heard her arouse from a day of drifting in and out of a stupor-like state. "You are in the County Hospital. You had an accident." Cece tried to reorient her. Julie was just beginning to remember the car that had been following her when her vehicle skidded off the road, everything was a blurr.

"I'm thirsty," Julie whispered.

"I'll get you some water." Her mom spoke softly as she gave Julie water with a straw. Julie sipped cautiously.

"Mom, you've got to contact Jay. I had some important papers with me in my car. Jay will need those. Please call him. Mom, I think I was being followed."

"Okay, let me go call him immediately!" Cece left the room to get a better phone signal. She walked to the outside of the hospital waiting area and dialed Jay's phone number. Finally reaching him, she was quick to share her good news that Julie was awake and speaking clearly, but yet still a little groggy, and weak.

"Hello Jay, Julie is awake now, and she needs to see you right away: it's important. She has information for you." She could also be in danger."

"I'll be right over, Cecilia, just keep her calm," Jay replied. He closed his phone, and hurried to his vehicle. · Returning to her daughter's room, Cecilia discovered an empty bed and disconnected I.V. "Nurse, nurse," she called, moving into the hallway. "Julie is gone." Having already searched the bathroom and nearby areas, her chest tightened. With heart racing and perspiration beads on her forehead, she couldn't keep tears from flowing as the nurse sought to locate the patient.

After further searching the room, the nurse quickly called security. She, then, called a Code 'Quick Step.'

◄━

As Jay was about to leave his office, his phone binged again. "Hello," Jay speaking."

Jay, Julie has been taken, or she left her room. Her belongings are here, but no Julie. I am terrified that she may have been abducted. I know security called the local police. Jay, please help." Cecilia cried.

What on earth, Cecilia? What could happen? She was still dazed, I'm sure. We'll find her. Try not to panic. I'm on it."

Jay promptly called Chief Jarod, but was soon to learn that the Chief had not had any word of the event, other than from the hospital of Julie's absence. Jay confided, "Jarod, please notify me of any updates on her whereabouts. I'm ill with worry. She may have been abducted You see, we were working on a case with confidential information that may be compromised by a foreign government."

"I'll be right on the case, and call in for other help, Jay."

"Thanks for your help. I'll be by to brief you more after my trip to the hospital. I must go now." He bid good day and closed his phone.

—◄◄

When Jay arrived to the hospital, he soon realized no witnesses. *Great.* He met Cecilia who sat in the lobby still with reddened eyes.

"Jay, I know Julie wasn't able to walk out alone. She was very weak." Jay tried to comfort her as tears flowed from her eyes again. Soon the security guards came by with puzzled expressions. "It looks as if someone should have noticed some commotion with this unusual carryout of an individual," the guards confided. Jay just stared, unable to find the right words.

"I'll stay with you, Cecilia, until the police arrive. He straightened his stance, trying to mask his fears. "Julie and I were working on a special assignment with the Herald when her accident occurred."

Julie's mom gasped, "I'm shocked. How could she just vanish, when she was barely conscious, Jay?"

Things happen when people desire information that isn't privileged, Cecilia."

Cecilia fought for control as tears continued.

"If I had not left the room, maybe this wouldn't have happened. I should have just waited about calling you until someone could stay with Julie. I'm somewhat to blame for this event," she cried.

"You know Chief Jarod and his officers will be here shortly, and I'll be helping. We'll find her." The files from Julie's car, he knew if the abductors knew he possessed them, they'd be after him too.

After careful consideration, Jay called back to the police station near West-End Hospital. "Lieutenant, let me speak with the Chief again, this is Jay."

"Yeah, hey Jay, Chief Jarod was on the phone, "What can I do for you, friend."

"Chief, don't turn over any belongings of Julie's to anyone. I'll go over details when I see you."

CHAPTER
SEVEN

J ulie almost choked with nausea: the meager sandwich and soup were tasteless. She was trembling with fatigue and hunger in the tiny room where her captors had her feet tied. Even her hands were tied when she wasn't eating. And, her wrists were excoriated. The ties were embedded into her flesh, so it seemed.

"How will I ever escape this entrapment?" She whispered.

She started to pray silently. *God, have mercy on me, and deliver me from this dreadful situation. You are my helper, in whom I trust. Father, you are ever near unto me.* Julie quoted scripture after scripture in her solitude; her lips trembled.

The journalist was attuned to the latest news updates on the T.V. across the hall. An alert was on the screen. She tried to focus her eyes from the bed in her unkempt room. I must be near the bay in Topeka, she concluded as she could barely see through the small window nearby. *I can detect the salt water the smell penetrates this cubicle. I'm not far away.*

How had her captors known that she was covering The Missing Witherton File assignment? She had only mentioned to two friends that she was headed out to determine Kevin's location.

Had Piareus, my coworker at the Herald, overheard anything? *Am I getting paranoid? I don't think so,* she tried to assure herself. I will definitely speak with Jay about these folks. She tried to quietly scour her memory. *Had Bill Finlay inside info?*

Her wandering thoughts were interrupted by Sovic. "The Russian, he sure speaks fluent English," she murmured. He kept showing up in her room with more troubling ideas.

"Julie, you sure are a beautiful woman to be involved in this escapade; it seems to be getting you into more trouble than you realize." Sovic sneered, as he straightened his stance. With his frayed open-collared shirt, rumbled trousers, and old brown hounds tooth jacket, he could never impress her. Even with his gothic face, his distasteful words and crooked teeth made his sculpted face look as if he had a bone to pick, and crabapples to fry.

"Don't you care that we could make your life much easier: if you'd just turn your files over to Jim and I. We heard about these files you obtained, from a reliable source (could be your own military), Ms. Julie. And, I could sure use your help in my connections to get the files to my government as I planned. Jim and I could make it well-worth your effort: both monetary-wise, as well as, with very comfortable living arrangements close to ours in Dagestan. We really live in an upscale area."

"Sovic, I have no desire to be a part of your plan to carry out this maneuver. Our country is above board in all endeavors to promote safety in any research or production involving our citizens, or others around the globe. So, back off."

"Now, now, Ms. Julie, you could be here for quite a while, if you continue with this lack of co-operation. Like I said, you could be an asset to us with your connections and journalism knowledge."

"What do you mean connections?"

"Well, you know, Finlay and your boss, are privy to many government personnel in the Ukraine and Dagestan."

"You can't mean Sayvinsky, he's an all American guy who has served this country well, even though born in Poland." Julie questioned the obvious insinuation.

"He certainly knows how to expedite travel from your country to ours, and how to get merchandise through security in many of your ports-a-call."

Julie had never imagined anything so absurd. Just wait 'til Jay got this news. He'd be able to sort it out. Maybe Federal agencies would need to be a part of this needed investigation. Worried lines were creeping upon her face, as she lay in her confinement: miserable, tolerating the abductors.

When the Russian turned and traipsed back toward his room, he called out in his deepest voice, "if you'll just tell us what we need to know, Ms. Julie, we might release you. We know the Lieutenant gave you some classified files, and he intended for us to locate you and grab those files. You were just a go between in this 'cat and mouse' game," Sovic chuckled as he turned and pranced back into her room.

"We saw Lieutenant Caleb meet you near Sandy Mountain. When we found him, he told us, with a little convincing on our part, you had those files we needed in your possession. We need those now, Ms. Julie! If you value your life, you'll co-operate. You understand?"

Sovic came near waving a knife. Squinting his left eye, as he was raging again, "you have a plenty to lose and very, very little to gain if you fail us."

"I'll try.." tears fell down her cheeks as she cringed in fear. "No need to get agitated. Get these ties off my wrist and I'll try to locate them. My car... I need to find it!" Julie fought to divert the tyrant. "I don't remember... Let me think. I skidded off the road." Sovic, did you bump the rear-end of my vehicle?"

He glared at her, "No, but I think you are imagining the collision," the Russian grumbled. Coming closer to her bed, he touched her face. She shrank her body state to avoid his touch.

"You need...to call the police. They may have my car: the files are probably ... *How did he know I really had the files?"*

"Whoa, No, wait a minute. You'll be the one to talk to the police. And you'd better be convincing that you just left the hospital with your brother to clear your mind and get some fresh air. Assure them that you're okay, and will pick up your belongings. Jim will be your guard, but just call him Neal, your brother, as you said, Ms. Julie; or, you may never see daylight again. Don't try any unusual games with us." He was ranting, his face red, and eyes engulfed with terror.

"We need those files. Jim and I were told that there's information in those that could benefit our government, and you can retrieve those for us." Sovic kept up the rant with a hands flailing. He reached for her as she tried to pull away.

Julie's wrists were hurting, crunched as she was. She knew Jay could help her to escape. *If I could just contact him-- Oh, how I wish I had a phone*, she fretted. "Sovic have you seen my phone."

"No, but you don't need to worry. Do you think we're amateurs? You know you're not calling anyone."

"Well, could you at least untie me? My circulation... and I'm in pain."

"Not until you can cooperate a little with us. Your time is running out," Sovic yelled. He limped back toward her again- exposing his knife. "Are you ready to talk to the police when I get them on the line, like I instructed? Or do you need some convincing?" Sovic jeered.

"Okay, okay! You need to calm down. If you'll get them on the phone line, and untie me." Sovic began to calm.

"Tell them that you and your brother, Neal, are coming to get your valuables tomorrow at nine o'clock: if that is a convenient time for them!" The Russian explained emphatically.

After Sovic dialed the police department, he handed the phone to Julie. She spoke with Chief Jarod, Jay's friend. She told him her needs and of her good health, and that she would arrive tomorrow with her brother to get her belongings.

◄◄

Chief Jarod immediately called Jay after he spoke with Julie. "Jay, Julie is arriving to get her belongings we're holding here. She'll be with her brother. Perhaps you should bring her briefcase and other papers for her. She avows she just needed a little rest, and time to gather her thoughts. Her brother arrived at the hospital and she left with him."

"Oh, no, Jarod, I'll be there myself to help you, and discuss this. And, Jarod, be prepared. She will have more company with her: those kidnappers who abducted her in the hospital. We need to be ready to capture them. It will not be Neal, Julie's brother. She's not with him. We need to get her free from the hands of the imposters who have her. I'll help you, Chief Jarod, and your officers any time that I can," Jay confessed.

"We could use you Jay, your investigative experience with the Sheriff's department was always commendable. Sheriff Jamison is assisting in our search. I'll get him to temporarily deputize you. I'll let you know when we're on the trail."

CHAPTER
EIGHT

J ay had a few minutes to check on Kevin's whereabouts as he waited for Julie's arrival. *I must try to determine if Kevin survived when his plane went down near Cuba.* He scrunched his lips while reviewing Julie's files more thorough again. He noted that Kevin had departed from Ramey Air Base in Aguadilla, Puerto Rico: a classified mission indeed.

Jay called the Commander at Ramey Air Base.

Commander Derrick answered, "Yes there was a Kevin who departed the base in route to Elgin Air Base near Florida, but only his Central Command knew his mission. Yes, I heard from the Swiss authorities yesterday that Cuban Coast Guard patrol had rescued Kevin from Cuban waters. I believe they said he had ejected from his aircraft and needed to get in touch with his Commander. He needed to notify him of his botched mission and downed plane."

Jay had obtained answers. But he needed more confirmation that Kevin was still alive. *What'll I tell Julie when I locate her. Will she be in shock? She must be close by and detained, or she'd surely find a way to contact me.*

"Commander, is Kevin injured, or ill since his

ordeal? I'm baffled about him, and his girl-friend who were in an auto accident recently? What information can I give her when I locate her whereabouts? Will he be released soon and flown back to his base? I understand from my research that he was a top Special-OP's, Lieutenant. I'm sure the Air Force needs his service now as never before."

"You are correct in that regard, but we must work through the Swiss channels to prove his intentions were not threatening to Cuba in any manner. He just had a fuel problem, and the fog compromised the other pilot's refueling efforts. I'm sure Kevin battled the ocean, weather elements, and other dangers just to get rescued. We're trying to gather all our resources to rescue him and his plane. We're convinced we'll overcome these stalled tactics of the Cubans, and get on with Kevin's release and our equipment returned to its storage facility."

"Commander, please keep us informed of how we are to be of service to you in the release of Kevin. His family and friends will be praying for him each day, and your military maneuvers in our nation's interest. We'll embrace the help of Kevin's Church to pray and contribute as needed to this cause. We, Americans, shall be a backbone of support when it comes to our soldiers, or their leaders in upholding our values either here or abroad."

Commander Derrick continued, "The Cubans told the Swiss personnel that they would detain Kevin until the U.S. confirmed his mission. Yes, to determine if it was a non-threatening flight assignment. Mr. Falk, the Cubans rebutted any remarks from the

Swiss Embassy, and argued they wanted facts, not just superfluous speculations."

The Commander was well briefed. "You people just need to assure the Cubans, via the Swiss, that we hold no enmity against their government," Jay said by phone. "And Commander, I understand the Cubans are very capable of negotiations when the outcome benefits them, as well as, the U.S. Don't you tend to agree?"

"Mr. Falk, don't ever doubt that we are on target with our plans to get Lieutenant Seals released. We need his help now as much as before he went down, if not more. Our situation with our nation's security is perilous, to say the least. If there is a way, we have the will, to secure his release as quickly as possible. And, Falk, let's keep this conversation confidential, for the benefit of all concerned. If I could cross the ocean now and rescue Lt. Kevin, I'd be on my way. It's that important to me and our base in Aguadilla. You stay in touch with me please, and I'll keep you and the family informed of all updates. We should negotiate his release soon."

CHAPTER
NINE

"**M**y Commander has no idea where I am," Kevin exclaimed to his Militia Officer. I need to call my Commander. He needs to assist me to retrieve my plane and get it to its final destination. I also need to notify my Command Center."

"The Swiss Government has already been in contact with us, Lieutenant. We need more information from you. We can't release you until we unravel your mission." Bonita explained. The dark skinned Hispanic was such a stocky, Senior Militia Officer: very smug indeed.

Lt. Seals continued to answer all inquiries with all the knowledge he could reveal to the Cuban authorities. Bonita, Senior Militia, wasn't convinced that Kevin was simply carrying technical supplies to Elgin Air Base. "For now, your plight is to remain in a Cuban jail cell, Lieutenant Seals. Alone." Bonita informed Kevin, in fluent English. Amazing.

No encouragement.

◄█

Kevin was confined in his jail cell for a week. I'm marking my days, and considering how I can get released. He kept his mind occupied and focused. *"I'm hungry, I had never dreamed that I would need you so, Father. I see how helpless I can be without your guidance and watchful eye in every aspect of my life. Stir me in the right direction, and plant my feet on solid ground. Near you, Lord. I am a believer, and my faith is in you. Be my protector and shield; and, Lord, keep me in the shelter of your wings, and I shall give you glory."*

A loneliness that he never thought possible casts shadows before his meek existence. He reminisced of days gone by spent with Julie on the beach in North Carolina, or touring the East Coast. Struggling to keep his mind occupied, though vision dim at times, he envisioned the cozy seaside restaurants along the way, especially The Clipper in Bernstein, North Carolina: that was his favorite.

If I could just contact her, I'm sure she would be receptive of my desire to see her, and be with her; as soon as I get released from this infested cubicle. I don't belong here, he almost shouted. *"It's repulsive!"* he mouthed. He was back in his cell after lengthy-grueling interrogations. *More prayers and confessions are sure to come. I'll get on my knees:* He bowed his head unsure of the words needed now.

Kevin began to call out, "where are you, Joe? I need you before I collapse. I'm depending on you this very minute."

"Can't you hear me? I need help. I'm starving.

And, Joe, I'm not a complainer. A swimming goldfish feeding on crumbs gets more protein and fat than I gather."

Joe sauntered into Kevin's cell arena with a slight wave of his arms. "I'se just serve-up whats they send me, K'vin. It's not my doing, this food service."

Kevin could feel the gnawing sensation rumbling in his gut. Pulling up his green-faded shirt, he stretched back to reveal his dwindling chest. "Can't you see my bones?" He spoke to Joe with a dry mouth.

Gawking at Kevin's bold display of his body, Joe emptied his pockets of crackers that he had accumulated over the past few days from the kitchen.

Joe, with his sleek-grayish hair, chiseled chin, and black eyes could always boost-up his mood a couple of notches. He was his most favored guard. Was he black, or a truly native Cuban? He sure sounded African-American. Finally, presenting his own meager rations of soup and crackers, he was pleasant. *I'm not sure if he is Hispanic; he speaks fair English.*

"When will this be all over, and me safely home, Joe?"

"You needs to be content, K'vin, 'tils we hear from your Commander. We needs to do some checking on your plane cargo that went down, Senor," Joe cautioned.

"We's planning on contacting your air base by ways of the Swiss authorities in two to three days. I's overheard some of the leaders talking. Maybe we'll hears what this dangerous flight of yours was abut. I'll sees you if I hear a squeak."

"Joe, could you get a letter out for me? I need to contact my folks and friends. I know you can help me. I see the 'cross' chain you're wearing. You must be a Christian, and you know how 'love thy neighbor as thyself.'"

"Sure, Kev'n, but I's also loyal to my employer. I need this job. But, if you'll gives me full cooperation, I might get one letter out without being discovered."

"Great, great, I'll have it ready by evening meal, if you can secure postage. We'll definitely deal?

Three weeks lapsed without any reply from home. "Joe, please, I need to hear from my family. Any mail I've missed?"

"No, but I check daily. Your letter was posted, I's unsure if you's get return."

The fourth week was upon him when Kevin noticed an envelope on his lunch tray. It was from his mom: She was so grieved to hear of Kevin's capture; but so relieved to get news of his whereabouts. If she could just hear from Julie, she would rest much easier. I don't know.. she stopped. But, I'm so happy that you're not injured and are safe at present, she wrote. Julie has been very busy with the Herald. I hope to hear from her soon."

Kevin was very anxious to hear from Julie. Something didn't sound right- that his mom had not heard from Julie. *I think I care more for her than I realized. If I could only see her, I know I would plan more for our future. I need Julie's love now more than ever. Did I say love? Yes, love. How can I plan in this dilapidated jail cell? Kevin fretted.*

Kevin sat down to write Julie's mom. Maybe I can get another letter out to be sure Cecilia is keeping close check on Julie. I know she would write me if she knew my circumstance. I can't imagine her being this occupied that she's not very concerned about me. He penned a letter to Cecilia.

Dear Cecilia,

Please be sure Julie is okay and not overworked. I'm sure she would write me. I need her support. I'm okay, but not happy. I'm working on a solution to this detainment.

Hope to hear from you and her soon.

My love to Julie and you,
Kevin

After completing the letter, Kevin would wait for Joe to come back, and he would give him the letter to mail. Perhaps a reply would be forthcoming in a few days. And, maybe, just maybe, Julie would reply this time after reading her mom's mail.

The days seemed longer each week as Kevin occupied his dismal surroundings. He could get little information about the Cuban Crisis situation that his Commander had discussed. He questioned Joe daily to gain some updates, but he would only comment, "our gov'ment only speaks of a U.S. threat of a military blockade- I's think that's a plan...

I don't know's details. It seems a lot of jabbering about Russia and our part in getting more supplies into our military.. I can't comment more. My lips are sealed..."

"Joe, surely you want peace and safety, don't you?"

"Sure, Kevin, but we's don't always have the goin's on here. Do you understand?"

"I do, Joe, but I know our country don't wish a build-up of warmongers in our back door either."

"What's that, Warmongers?" I've never heard that mentioned? Is that a bad word? I's not understand." "Listen to me, Joe. I believe you know more than you admit. You must know the United States desires peace, but we won't be threatened by Russian armament that could eventually annihilate us. We desire better relations with Cuba, but we stand firm on our word and principals. That's all I'll say for the present..."

"Gracias, Senor, I's believe in brotherly love. And you's a Christian, isn't that a fact? I's believe we's need to pray for our leaders and country: God can work miracles."

"That's true, Joe. But, God expects us to defend ourselves if the need arises. Don't you agree?"

"O'yes! Yes. I must get our trays, and be off now. Let's pray each day and night."

"Exactly, Joe."

Joe departed his cell without further words.

The next day Kevin sought more time in prayer, but even time alone with God brought little comfort from the heat of the day, the loneliness, and the hunger pains he endured. The way, the truth, and the life, seemed very distant as the long dreary days dragged by with scanty food, and filthy surroundings. His bright moments were when Joe, his guard, would saunter in with his food and water... like the present.

"You's still holding-on to your faith and hope, Kevin?" Kevin raised his head and eyes toward Joe, as if to rebuff his comment, but only slowly responded. "I'll keep on, keeping on- as long as I have a breath, Joe. I have folks who love and care for me. And, a God, who's my shield and fortress. Just keep me in your prayers also."

"I's certainly canst do that for you," Joe replied. You pray for my wife... she's not well. We are low on funds, and she needs to see her doctor. We need much prayer and help. My brothers try to help, but they're in need also. We just get by day by day with our meager moneys. Life is not an easy road here in Cuba. Many people are in need, but our gov'tment.is not helping with our economy. And, our people are suffering with lack of jobs."

"I have plenty of time as my days are long, Joe, I'll pray for you and family, and our countries. Maybe, there will be relief soon. God is still on the throne and cares for his own. We must keep our faith. O'for better days. Good day, Joe."

"Same to you Kev'n"

"When Kevin was alone again, he knelt in prayer. He prayed not only for Joe and his family, but also for his family and beloved friends. Somehow, God would see him through this ordeal. He had sent him a Christian guard to ease his discomfort, and he knew He would be with him each grueling day. "He is my light in the darkness of each day." As he closed in prayer, his thoughts were on Julie, and their families. He must try to come up with a plan for God to help him out of confinement. His next prayers would be in pleas for life out of bondage. He would never give in, to this cell being his destiny. Tomorrow would be a new day. He would practice his faith, but also seek God's help.

As the lights were dimmed that evening in his cell, Kevin could only exercise, read, write, or pray. His day had been spent much the same as every day. Except today, had been more prayerful. There seemed to be a veil of peace overcoming his soul. The evening was quiet, not even the commotion from the inmates with yells and discontent. Kevin opened his journal and recalled Joe's visits; he had recorded conversations from fellow inmates about the Catholic priests who occasionally visited.

Kevin decided suddenly, "I shall inquire with Joe tomorrow of how I might solicit help from the Church. Yes, that is a good plan!" As he began to doze, his mind had gathered more hope and courage for an intervention in his demise...

He awakened early the next morning to a small ray of sunshine bursting through the tiny window of his cell. The penetration of light and warmth swept through his body like a vibrant current of hope. A well-spring of joy sparked his mood. He could hardly wait to tell Joe of his ideas, or was it a dream - that had come from afar... Regardless, he would attend to the recognition of how God could move in his life. Now, he must pursue the plan with Joe, and not grow weary in his determined plans to seek

God's help to obtain freedom again. "God has other tasks for me. I have a future mapped out before the foundation of the world. I need to give ear, heart, mind, soul, and strength to my calling."

CHAPTER
TEN

Five weeks lapsed. Kevin was growing weary of his time in seclusion in his Cuban cell when he received word on Tuesday of a possible planned visit from some Swiss dignitaries. He was hoping to get some helpful information concerning his release from his tight cubicle. If Commander Derrick could show 'just cause' for his flight path aversion due to weather conditions, he might fantasize his release. He was leery of too much optimism for fear he'd be let down.

Kevin stayed very tense most of the morning awaiting news. Mid-afternoon came around without a dribble of news. Finally, at six p.m. when dinner arrived, Kevin halted the guard with his face ablaze with worry. "Joe, I need to see my visitor that was to arrive today."

"I haven't seen anyone come by. Maybe it was a cruel hoax. Just give me a few minutes and I'll check it out."

Joe left the confines of the jail to try to gather information regarding any visitors to the area. He was friends with many of the security officers, and could blend in rather well while he pre-tended to complete his detail in the Cuban cell area.

When the guard came back, he revealed, "Someone came by, but security wasn't ready for thems to visit. Maybe theys will secure a release for you when an individual theys trust vouches for you with a message they wish to hear, or they determine your plane's cargo. Perhaps your Defense Department could influence them."

"Joe, you know our government only speaks through Swiss channels, and that is limited in nature."

"Well, Kev'n, if the Swiss Embassy would show their true colors, they could get the needed info and provide convincing documents to secure your release. Patience, prayer, and determination are the keys. Remember, God is all powerful and mighty. Hopefully, they can strike a deal."

This is Joe talking. He's a foreigner, but a fellow Christian. I must keep the faith even when I'm severely tested. Kevin's focus was changing. Courage and hope were beginning to be rekindled. Maybe he could get a little sleep tonight for a change. He had not received any word from home or Julie. He knew she had some crucial assignments in her work that she had been concerned about. He longed to hear from her. He hoped the food would improve, even though, Joe was bringing bread crumbs it seemed.

The next day with a meager breakfast of gruel and bread, Kevin questioned, "Joe, I appreciate all you've done for me, but I have heard rumors from some of the other detainees that the Catholic church has, on occasions, assisted U.S. prisoners of faith who were wrongfully kept in Cuba. Could you please check with the Church and determine if they could intercede on my behalf? I'm innocent, Joe! My plane just missed it's refueling deliverer. I was out of fuel! I had no choice but to eject from my plane: it was going down. If I landed in forbidden territory, what else could I do to get to safety?"

"Okay, okay, Kev'n! I'll checks with my church and try to get something going. If you will promise to contact my aunt in Miami, when and if you get released, maybe I can pull some strings. Aunt Cornelia can assist me to get the needed funds for my wife's surgery this month."

"I will do anything that I possibly can to get to her. Give Me her phone number and locale, and help me to get out of here! Oh, and write her a note of your needs and intentions," Kevin smiled.

"Then, Kev'n, I will make my church contacts as soon as possible," Joe confessed.

Kevin gave Joe the name of his home church in Kansas. He decided he must trust someone, even if a risk.

"Hopefully, my church can assist in prayer, and or, funds if needed for my release. I am innocent of any crime, Joe. I shall be eternally grateful if you can get this release process moving. Joe, I'm dwindling before your eyes. As Christians, we should help one another regardless of our government issues." Kevin was crying out to his only contact who might help.

CHAPTER
ELEVEN

Julie was in route with her companion, Neal(aka, Jim) to the West-End police station in hopes of procuring her files to her captors. *Not my desire, to say the least,* she muttered.

Surely Jay has not brought the files with him to the West- End police, she considered. He knows we can't turn over the files to these thugs. Her captor, she knew was armed with his weapons inside his vest and boot. And, she knew there was to be a back-up captor, Sovic, in the van outside the building.

What would she do if shots were fired at her or Jay. If I could just get word to him? Julie knew being a former policeman, Jay would be prepared to aid her if he only knew her dire need. She began to silently pray: *O' God, please be with me and my rescuers at this perilous time. God, you know we have a mission to do for our country. Protect us, and use us to help our warriors in the service of our country. We stand in awe of your greatness and power.*

Julie bit her lip, and clasped her hands tightly to keep them from shaking. The closer they came to the police station, the more difficult it seemed to keep her hands from trembling.

Nine o'clock was approaching. Julie and her cohorts were arriving at the police station. All seemed quiet as they approached. The entrance was occupied with visitors, but Chief Jarod met them at the door.

Julie was quick to greet the Chief. "Hello, Chief Jarod, this is my brother, Neal, and I am Julie Peterson, if you recall. I've been at Neal's house getting some needed rest for the past few days; trying to clear my head from my accident. Have you any news about who may have caused the plunge? I sure need some answers about my car, and how I landed down a ravine and into a tree."

"I have not received any more details, Julie. But I do know where your vehicle is being kept. We sure were worried about you. Have you contacted your mom?" Chief Jarod questioned.

"No, Sir, I lost phone in the chaos, and I haven't thought to ring her number. In fact, I can't remember her number. Could you write it down for me."

"Sure thing, Julie."

"Nice to meet you, Neal. You must live close by. You two just come into my office and we'll go over some events. Then, I'll get your belongings, Julie." Jarod smiled warmly. You can contact your mom if you would like, Ms. Julie." Chief Jarod swung the door wide as he retrieved Cecilia's phone number.

After she called her mom, the Chief tried to reassure her that the investigation would continue regarding her accident, and more details were coming. He mentioned his concern for her welfare and safety as tears begin to pool in her eyes.

"Julie, your friend from work is here. He sure is anxious to hear from you." The Chief called for Jay to come to his office.

Julie's eyebrows were raised at this revelation. *What was about to transpire? Would Jay be able to help secure her freedom? Her hands began to shake as she began to silently pray, Lord, I need you, O'how I need you;* the song she remembered from church had developed into a prayer. Her heart was open to God's protection, his divine power and faithfulness, even though she couldn't control her tremors.

As Jay entered the office to meet Julie and her guard, Neal, he stopped, "Hold it right there," Jay and the other officers met Neal with guns pointed at Julie's guard. The guard immediately pulled Julie in front of him. He shielded himself from any approach with his gun pulled and pointed at her back.

"Stop, and drop your guns, or Julie gets the bullets," Neal yelled.

Jay immediately dropped his weapon, as did the other officers.

Why have I been so vulnerable? Surely I can escape. Julie quivered with fear as Neal tugged at her waist.

Jay had recently heard that the culprit in this siege of the suspected van outside had been injured in his van: he was in custody. He was wary of Neal's escape as he was backing out toward the entrance door of the police station with Julie in his grasp. Suddenly Neal threw open the door. He was then grabbed by two policemen who were crouched and waiting outside the entrance door. As one officer grabbed Neal from behind, he knocked his weapon upwards disarming the kidnapper. The weapon fired as it spiraled, but fortunately no one was injured.

◄◄

Julie was safely rescued, and her captors were both now in custody. An ambulance was called for Sovic, and he was transported to the West-End Hospital with his police guards. The injured officer, who had confronted Sovic, rode with a rescue squad that had been called earlier for his treatment.

Jay immediately came to comfort Julie near the entrance. She had developed a headache, but was aghast with relief that No one else was injured. "Julie, your files are safe, Jay assured her. "You're going to see some feathers fly now, Julie. These guys shall not go unpunished, I promise you."

"Come into my office, Julie, and give us a briefing on all you've heard and endured these past few days. Chief Jarod spoke with compassion to Julie; I know you're not well after all you've experience my dear, but we must arrest these dudes as soon as they're able for a jail cell. It seems they will be hospitalized for a few days."

Jay departed to bring back coffee and Danish for Julie, himself, and Jarod. Julie paused to call her mom. She could hardly speak while shaking from the ordeal. As she tried to calm herself, the Chief assured her that they would protect her. Finally, she relived and reviewed the past few days' events as best she could. "Jay, I just wished I had called you before I headed to the mountains. I knew better.

I thought time was the essence, and overlooked the safety factor. Please forgive me," she cried.

"Julie, it would have made little difference to these hoodlums. They're getting paid to disrupt the U.S. defensive plans. We must take more precautions, therefore," Jay conveyed.

Later in the day as Jay was escorting Julie to her mom's, Jay mentioned the files. "Julie, we must deliver your files that I obtained from your wrecked vehicle to the proper personnel at the Defense Department. We'll obtain a police escort to help as soon as possible. And, it is imperative that we try to secure Kevin's release from the jail cell in Cuba where he is being detained."

Julie gasped. She didn't realize that Kevin had been captured by the Cubans. "Is he safe? Is he injured? Why is he in Cuban custody?"

"I'm sorry Julie. His plane ran low of fuel and he had to eject over Cuban waters. I thought you... knew...," he almost choked. He was rescued by Cuban Coast Guard, and turned over to the Cuban Militia. He is being held until the Cuban authorities determine his plane's cargo, and his mission." Jay grimaced as he spoke knowing the hurt and worry this would bring Julie.

"Whoa... this is too much for me in one day," she cried.

Jay stopped the car, still trying to console Julie. "Others in our government are desperately trying to get him released."

"I just can't imagine what he must be enduring now, as well as, when he plunged into the Caribbean. We must start our strategy today to get him home," Julie surged as she spoke. I never dreamed I'd be faced with this after my kidnapping. Please just stop the car, and let's get something to drink. I don't care if it's just lemonade, I need a refreshment and time to think. I don't want my mom to see me this distressed. I've got to pull myself together before we reach her house."

"Julie, and Jay, so good to see you both! I've been very worried for your safety." Hugging each of them, she ushered them out to the deck. The gentle evening breeze brought a sigh, a relief to Julie. As she sought the wicker cushioned chair next to Jay, she stumbled into the seat.

"O' dear, Julie, I see you've lost a few pounds. Please tell me what happened? Where, oh where, have you been?" Cecilia glanced from one to the other. Tears began to cloud Julie's eyes, and she choked to get a word out...

Finally.

"M..om..., I've had a terrible experience. I was abducted from the hospital, and kept captive by some, I think Russian thugs."

"O' my, your wrist, Julie? I must care for you. Her mom carefully grasped her wrist. "And, I see you need some of my good cooking. You need to stay with me awhile to regain your strength, weight, and dignity again!"

"Jay, how did this happen to my darling?" You both have a great deal of explaining to give me. But first, I need to see to you both some good nutrition this minute." Cecilia commented, while hurrying back to her kitchen.

Julie called out to her Mom. "Have you heard from Kevin?"

"I did receive one letter. I've just been appalled at his circumstances, but I couldn't get in touch with you, Julie. I didn't confide about your absence to him since he was under stress in Cuban confinement. I'll show the letter once I get you nourished, but he said he wasn't injured. I'm not sure if he ever received my letter, Julie," Cecilia spoke from the door.

"It's okay, Mom. I knew you'd do what was best for him. Mom, let's all be in prayer continually for Kevin. We'll need to involve our church also. Next, I would like some good food," Julie confessed, smiling all the while."

"I'll see to it right away, Dear." Cecilia headed back to the kitchen.

While enjoying the fragrance of tulips, daffodils, etc. of her mom's garden, Julie began to unload her concerns to Jay about Sovic, one of her captors. "He mentioned Sayvinsky, our boss, and others at the Herald assisting the Russians with import and export of merchandise to and from their country."

"Julie, there may be some ties between these folks, and our Sayvinsky, that we're unaware of. I'll get right to the center of this with Chief Jarod. We'll investigate. In the meanwhile, just lay low on this, and don't stir-up any unusual concerns at work."

"Don't worry, Jay, I don't wish any more scary situations."

"Just let Jerome know you need a few days off, Julie."

"Okay, Jay. I'm a little tired. Are you staying for dinner? Mom is baking a roast as I speak, and I'm sure she'll include great veggies with it. Maybe even an apple cobbler to top off dessert."

"Oh, Julie, that sounds great, but I must be on my way. I'll see you early tomorrow. Hopefully, we can finish this intriguing assignment, all but the fine print, and notify others to sum-up the investigations: especially, the Feds.

As Jay left Cecilia's house, he contacted Chief Jarod. "Hey Chief, I need a special favor. Julie's info about Sovic and his cohorts need a little more delving into."

"Yes, Jay. What's the idea. I wasn't aware of others beyond those mentioned involved in Julie's case. Of course we are checking Sovic's connections.'' Jarod stated.

"Julie mentioned that Sovic spelled out some names of individuals at the Herald where she works. I need you to contact Special Ops, or someone in the CIA who might do a little more detailed investigation on the kidnapper's contacts here in the U.S. I think Julie's captors received more knowledge base from persons where she is employed." Jay was emphatic.

"Okay, Jay, I'll get on this. You can brief me more when you're by the office. You can drop by anytime that it is convenient for you."

Jay and Julie were off early Tuesday morning in route to their contact with the U.S. Defense Department. They hoped to get the Witherton Files back to General Faust of the department. The detective escort was fortunately on time for their personal protection. Travel seemed safe thus far. No sign of being tailed.

When they reached their destination, Jay called the contact, General Seth Faust, to verify a safe delivery of the classified files in their possession.

"General Faust, speaking. Yes, Jay, I am awaiting you and Julie. I can assure you the files will be safely stored again! We've had an investigation here of all personnel in our Defense Records Department, and there have been two employee's released. I understand there's been one released also at the Herald. This screening should prevent any potential leaks coming in or out of this office. There will be an on-going investigation to prevent classified files landing in the wrong hands. Rest assured that we are being thorough in our security: it has been beefed-up in all aspects of confidential information movement at our facility. What is your expected time of arrival? I'm sure you have your own protection with you. But, there's always some extra military guards in this locale, and we'll be ready for you when you arrive."

"We're arriving outside the building as I speak, General." As Jay bade good-day and closed his phone, they exited the SUV. The detective then escorted Julie and Jay to General Faust's office. They were indeed pleased to turn-over the Witherton Files to the General. After greetings and handshakes, Jay was the first to mention Julie's daring experience with Sovic and his cohorts.

"General Faust, have you heard of all the dangers involved with Julie in returning these classified files to you? Have you heard that the Russians may have some knowledge of your records placement in this area?"

"Yes, Jay, I know anything is possible, but I can assure you, they don't have any details or specifics of our classified data. We have only limited data or content of our military files stored anywhere near our personnel. Our secured files are not easily accessed, and our personnel must have security clearance. But, since suspicions were aroused, we've updated our program."

"It helps to know the details of our military's classified files are not compromised to foreign governments. Julie and I would rest better knowing our efforts to help were worthwhile. Do you think our personal safety can be achieved, now that we've accomplished our mission?" Jay queried.

"That should not be a problem, Jay, now that we are in control of our potential leaks. Just continue to be cautious until you're sure of those associated with Sovic and his felons are captured. Be diligent."

"O', by the way, did the Feds clear the officers in our military who tried to further protect our files due to Russian scrutiny: by releasing classified files to Julie?" Jay asked.

"That process is being finalized, Jay. Our investigators should tie up all the loose ends. Yes, we know who was behind the movement of our records, and we shall be working on all details of Julie's accident with the aid of other law enforcement. We shall penetrate the wall of resilience to protect our staff and others involved wherever located."

Faust spoke with determination to resolve enigmatic issues,

"Well General, keep everything safe. We'll be returning to Topeka today. Good day, Sir. Jay and Julie smiled as they bade General Faust goodbye.

Julie was relieved to arrive home. As she entered her mom's driveway that afternoon, she sighed deeply. Her thoughts were of Kevin. She whispered, "I long for his return home. He has succumbed to enough turmoil, similar to some of mine. How shall I explain the endangerments I've encountered, she mused. 'O will I have tales to tell our children; I should've kept a diary.

Julie was at her mom's when the Herald contacted her. She was delighted to tell them that the Classified Files had been safely secured. "Jerome, I should have you a complete report, and news brief on how they were recovered when Jay and I return to the Herald tomorrow."

"The Russian government may have some explaining to do in regard to some of their activities here in the States." Julie informed Jerome.

"What are you saying, Julie?"

"I'll tell you more tomorrow, Jerome," Julie quirked before saying, "I must go," then silencing her phone.

Cecilia's heart was filled with warmth and gladness each time her daughter joined. With the aroma of fresh coffee, cookies, scones, and apple turnovers wafting near Julie's nostrils, she began to perk-up.

"Mom, we did get our files back safely to their owner, and I feel safer now that our assignment is over. Life should be better with the thugs arrested, or detained by police authorities. Help me to continue to pray for Kevin, Jay, and myself," Julie pleaded.

"I shall be in prayer for all of us, Julie. I never dreamed our family would be subjected to this kind of danger."

"Well, Mom, don't fret. We shall now strive to remember and face each day, 'with God on our side, who can stand against us.'" Julie begged to stand firm.

"Julie, I am so relieved that you are a daughter of faith." Cecilia embraced her with love and soothing words.

After a night of peaceful sleep, Julie arose to streams of sunlight as she opened the drapes in her room. Downstairs to the kitchen, she was happy to be returning to work. After a light breakfast with her mom, she rushed to her room to quickly dress, and was off to work.

◄◄

Arriving at the Herald office, Julie bit her lower lip and tilted her head back. Bracing herself, she greeted her fellow employees.

"Hey, Julie. Good to see you back. Did you know we have some new employees? And Bill Finlay and Sayvinsky are no longer with us. Come meet the newest members of our team," Jerome sought to make her feel at ease. "Your new boss, Phil Connor, and team member, Cal Lindberg. They were transferred to us from the Iowa office. I'm sure Jay knows these tenured guys."

"Happy to meet you all. Glad to be back, and anxious to get abreast of all the new developments," Julie said.

"Ms. Julie, come into my office," Jerome announced. "Seems you've had a few dips into some deep water while away… -without a paddle. We know that Finlay and Sayvinsky are under close scrutiny by the Feds. Their connections with Sovic and his cohorts are in question. They shall be detained by Federal authorities until their part in your capture has been defined. Any criminal activity will be punished," Jerome assured Julie. "Whether Sovic acted alone, or with his government is to be determined. In the meanwhile, neither Sayvinsky nor Finlay shall return to this office."

"Julie, I think you shall enjoy working with our new boss, Phil Connor. Being from Iowa, Jay should be aware of his capabilities. Feel free to assist us in our many developments that we are pursuing. We'll strive to push the Herald forward."

"Jerome, thanks for your confidence in me. Perhaps you have already heard of Kevin, my friend, and his downed plane. I know he was able to eject from it, but he was captured by the Cubans. I'm hoping that he'll be released soon. I should get some details surrounding his capture, endangerment, and release, in the near future. I've been praying daily..". Julie started to tear-up as she spoke.

"Julie, let us know if we can assist anyway. We are here to help." Jerome spoke with compassion as he strode over to comfort her. We appreciate all your extra efforts in the recovery of the missing Witherton Files. I know you'll be rewarded soon."

CHAPTER

TWELVE

Kevin's commander in Puerto Rico was anxious to get him released from his jail cell in Cuba, and to see to his plane recovered. If his plane could not be retrieved, the Air Force needed to recover his sunken warhead that was aboard the plane. This should be accomplished before any intervention by the Cuban government was planned. Colonel O'Neal was not enjoying the stalling tactics of the Cubans in releasing Officer Seals, one of his top-gun pilots. Standing only five feet eleven inches, he could carry his weight and muscular physique. With stern eyes and a passion of grace equal to any of the Commanders at the Aguadilla Air Base, O'Neal had firm convictions. Besides, it was 1962, and Cuba was gaining more establishments with the Russians day by day.

Speaking with the Swiss Authorities, O'Neal questioned, "What was Fidel thinking: we'd look the other way?" With Cuba's stiff penalties for Americans found in their waters, O'Neal was concerned for Kevin's safety, and his downed plane's retrieval. "We need both pronto!" He reminded the Swiss as he negotiated to get Kevin released." I think we are just going in circles with this situation. I have all the documents from the U.S. government needed to clear him from any wrong-doing. His fuel just ran out, that is the only, I repeat, the only reason, he had to disengage from his plane!" Still speaking with the Swiss Embassy, O'Neal reiterated the importance of Kevin's release. "We need him back at the Command Center Post in Puerto Rico as soon as possible to resume his duties. And, his family needs him. His mom, Jacqueline, suffered a heart attack a few days ago, and she is in serious condition in the CCU unit at her local hospital. She is stable now, but very weak."

Cuban Colonel Petros responded to his contact with the Swiss after Commander O'Neal had silenced his phone. "I know the Catholic Church here and Padre Carlos are striving to get Kevin released to you in a few days. The Swiss Embassy could facilitate this endeavor if they could meet the church plane with the proper documents at a destination near Elgin Air Base. We could plan a rendezvous with them with Fidel's approval to expedite his release... if he is innocent. His arrival in Puerto Rico could be within a few days; then, he could be back to his mom's bedside," he chuckled." The Swiss, then, notified O'Neal that plans were progressing to get Kevin home.

One week later, Kevin was released from Cuba and on a Catholic Church plane to a destination at Elgin Air Base. With the Swiss authorities aboard the plane, they were also able to transfer the proper documents to the Cubans: these authenticated Kevin's innocence of any criminal intent. Lieutenant Seals would now be free to obtain a flight back to Puerto Rico.

Colonel O'Neal was relieved to see Lieutenant Seals two days later at Ramey Air Base. His debriefing was quickly underway. Trying to determine Kevin's downed plane's locale was of utmost importance. And why had his refueling plane missed it's point of contact? These factors must be addressed. Next a team must be sent to recover the cargo, or whatever was required to make it inoperable.

Three days later, a team was dispatched to recover Kevin's plane's cargo and airlift it safely to a ship en route to Elgin Air Base. Much sonar equipment and other supplies needed for the recovery effort were dispersed with the team to the Caribbean.

Fortunately, the team was able to get sonar signals from the downed plane just outside Cuban waters. Being in the United States territorial waters, should make the recovery process safe and away from Cuba's grasp of the sunken vessel. Now there should not be interference from anyone. This gave the courageous rescue personnel more confidence of the cargo's retrieval.

Five hours into the search, Colonel O'Neal secured a call from his team that they were getting near the ship. Their capabilities were such that they should be able to uplift the cargo to the rescue ship. The plane with cargo was outside Cuban waters. And, it's cargo should be retrieved and delivered by rescue ship to the Elgin Air Base near Florida the same day.

The retrieval of the plane's cargo was a tremendous victory for the rescue team, and for the United States. Kevin was very pleased to hear of the miraculous recovery. The team was commended for their skill and technology. The effort was of utmost importance as a future benefit to the nation's security.

"Kevin, now you'll be able to leave for the United States to check on your mom, and be at her bedside." Colonel O'Neal graciously informed him. "And, Lieutenant, we did a little follow-up on your refueling plane's whereabouts during your flight emergency near Cuba. The pilot was required to turn back to avoid disaster himself. The fog and weather conditions prevented him from reaching you. His radio was fouled, which hindered his communication with you; thus, your botched mission. Sorry, Son, but there are never any guarantees of weather conditions. I'll hope planning and communications are much better next time."

Colonel O'Neal was frequently referring to his recruits as Son. Kevin knew this was just his way of showing his concern for all involved in Special Ops missions, and his passion for getting to the root of any problems which came up with his men in uniform.

"Well," Kevin slowly confided, "it would be an asset if traffic control could assist a little in advance of declining weather conditions. Anyway, I'm relieved to be going to check on Mom. Sure hope she is improving."

CHAPTER
THIRTEEN

The morning came with a burst of sunshine filling the cozy muted-gray bedroom at Julie's mom's. She stretched and remembered the warmth, love, and security that she'd embraced growing up as a child in this home. Recalling how her mom and dad always encouraged and promoted her in seeking the best life had to offer, helped her to continue her journalism career at one of the most prestigious journalism schools in Topeka. Often she was eager to show them just how far she had come. Except of late, life had been a little challenging: what with her kidnapping, endangerments, etc...

Julie's thoughts were interrupted by her phone pinging almost as soon as her alarm clock buzzed.

"Hello, Julie sweetheart," Kevin greeted, scarcely giving her time to say hello. "I'm going to be home in a few days from the service," he choked-up speaking with elation.

Julie couldn't believe her ears. Could this be Kevin? She could hardly get her breath, Her heart kept skipping beats as she fought to contain her emotions. She had often in her prior days been planning her response to his calls, but quickly began-

"O', Kevin! It's really you! Are you okay? I heard about your plane going down. Are you suffering any deleterious effects from your harrowing escape into Cuban territory," Julie questioned."

"I'm doing fine now that I'm speaking to the one I have been missing so these past few weeks. It is great to hear your voice. I need to not only hear you, but see your beautiful face (the one molded perfectly with your lustrous brown hair, and cameo skin.) "Julie shivered to hear those words. She sat down and grabbed a tissue to wipe her teared-up eyes. The words would not come…

"Julie, my mom is ill, and I'm coming home as soon as arrangements can be made. I've been confined in Cuba, but I'm back at my base now. I'll tell you all about it when I get home."

Finally, her voice returned. "Kevin, I've missed you terribly. And, I've been extremely worried about your safety."

"Julie, I can imagine, but I'm okay. We have a lot of catching-up to do. I need to get busy and book my flight."

"Good, Kevin, have a safe flight. I hope to see you soon. Call me as soon as you have the details: I'll be close by." Julie was ecstatic and rushed to tell her mom.

"Mom, Mom," she yelled storming thru the kitchen door.

Kevin is coming home. He's coming home, Mom."

Cece embraced her, "I'm overwhelmed with delight, Love."

Kevin arrived at Julie's mom's two days later with news that his mom, Jacqueline, was some better, but still remained in the hospital. "She is to have a cardiac catheterization tomorrow, Julie. I hope you can come with me to the hospital, and stay until I hear the cath. results. I'll be quite anxious."

"Kevin, I'll call Phil at the office now, and I'll plan to go with you. I'm sure Connors will be happy for me to accompany you at this time. I'm thrilled you are safely home. You and I must rejoice that we are both uninjured. You know, I have much to tell you also. I have not had a picnic while you were away. Let's just allow Mom to compliment us with her Chinese cuisine while we do some catch-up on our daring escapes and rescues: your botched mission and my compromised assignments."

Kevin's smile dwindled at Julie's words. What was his favored girl about to reveal? Had he missed out on more than he realized? And, why was she staying at her mom's instead of at her place?

Cecilia entered the living room to announce that dinner was underway. "Kevin, so great to see you." She embraced him as she greeted. "Are you doing well or just recuperating?"

Cecilia commented while embracing Kevin.

"Actually, Cecilia, I did lose some sleep, and a great deal of weight. But, I'm thankful for God's help, and all the prayers being lifted on my behalf. God is so good, and his mercy endured with me."

"Dear Son, you know who is, who was, and who is to come. Your faith is self-evident in the way you walk and talk. I'm glad you seem to live out your faith instead of just speaking of it. God surely knows your heart and what his plan is for you. Just keep the faith. You know Julie has mentioned your love for God many times to me," Cecilia commented. "Now we see your true colors. Good to have you home again. And, Kevin, we're praying for your mom daily." Cecilia strode into the kitchen after her comments to finish preparing dinner.

Julie's phone rang as she embraced Kevin with enduring intent. As Kevin's lips reached hers, she quivered at his touch. Her phone rang as she was enjoying the moment: she allowed it to ring several times- hoping for a wrong number. Finally, she reached for the phone. "Hello, Jay. What's happening?"

"Julie, I've got more news," Jay spoke.

"Can it wait? I'm quite busy. You know I need a little down time after all the events we've had to cover lately. It would be great if this news could be held until morning."

"I need your input on what to think of Sovic's death? He has just expired at the hospital." Jay spoke and sounded vexed.

"Umm, I thought he was a viable ruffian whose blood wouldn't be staunched regardless of his ferocious behavior. I'm sorry if I sound defensive, but I endured some pain from his terrorizing me. I'll get with you as soon as I can, and we'll go over this. Kevin's here, and I need this time with him today."

Good, I'll see you early a.m. at the Herald? We can work on this new development. Okay?"

"Oh no, Jay, I'm to go with Kevin to see his mom tomorrow. She is having a heart cath... Maybe we can talk in the afternoon, if all goes well."

"That will be fine. I can meet you all at the hospital coffee shop if you will call me as soon as you are free to talk."

"Sounds like a good plan. And, Jay speak with Jerome at work. He needs to be aware of Sovic's departure. The Feds... do they need to know?" Julie suggested.

"Julie," Kevin interrupted. "What is this about?" His curiosity was obvious.

"Jay, I must go." She silenced her phone.

"Kevin, I have so much to tell you. I'll just start begin to tell you of when I was abducted, and share the story about my kidnapping, auto accident, and other traumatic events while you were away. Sovic was one of my kidnappers. He has expired in the hospital. He was not very kind to me (keeping me tied-up as he did...)" Julie went on and on as to her trying experiences. "But, Kevin, I really don't wish you to be bothered with details. I'm safe now, and hope to stay that way."

"I'm so sorry you had to suffer these endearments, Julie. I wish I could've been here for you: to comfort and support you. It seems we both have been exposed to close encounters these last few weeks. I have a few days off, and I'd like to spend much of that time with you." Kevin's care and compassion were on display.

"Kevin, I'll be with you as much as I possibly can, but I must be back at work, I've been off too much already. Even though my time off was unavoidable, I have some catch-up to do." "I understand, Julie. Could we have dinner out tomorrow night if Mom is okay?"

"Yes, I'd love to, Kevin. I have so much to discuss with you," Julie acquiesced. "We need our time to discuss our plans and how we are to continue to pray for our future. I need some time to decompress, but my duty calls- to my work and my family life. With you home and near me, I feel like I can get back to my norm. This fear I've had must stop," she sighed.

***

While Kevin and Julie were at dinner the next evening, he kept mentioning how great Jackie was with his Mom. Julie just listened with interest. She wondered why he had never mentioned her before. Why had Jackie not visited his mom while she was in the hospital? Maybe she was imagining things, but he sure seemed to have a keen interest in Jackie. Well, she wasn't going to draw-up any wrong conclusions.

When Julie dropped Kevin off at his Mom's later that night, Jackie met him at the door. Julie didn't know if Kevin's sister was still there, or had she gone home? Julie just drove on home after their goodnights, but, still... wondering about the events. "I'll question him later," she decided.

While in prayer that night, she prayed that God would give her discernment to all the mysteries in her life, and guide her footsteps. Would there ever be any guarantees in her work or relationships? She harbored some doubts.

Jay called her shortly after her prayers. "Julie, I have some news," he exclaimed.

"Yes, Jay, what is it?"

"I've heard from Jarod. He has news from the Feds.

There may be a connection between the guy visiting Sovic, and the guy who bumped your car. They're checking his vehicles for signs of any damage or paint smears on any of them. We may know something soon, Julie. Keep your hopes up, and continue in prayer for closure to some of our experiences."

"Yes, Jay, it seems I'm doing a lot of that lately. *See you at work tomorrow. Jay was doing follow-up on her case..*

◄◄

Jay met Chief Jarod at the West-End hospital the next day. "Someone may have visited Sovic before he expired. Someone may have heard or seen something suspicious. He was doing better. I know he had good security, but the more leads we have, the better the prospects for uncovering any foul play, Jarod."

"I fully agree, Jay," Jarod volunteered.

Jay and Jarod were met at the hospital by a crew of reporters. They had hoped to evade questions. "Okay, guys, we're in the dark on how Sovic's condition changed so suddenly. All we can do is interview visitors and staff for now." Jay tried to stay a step ahead of the traffic.

Excusing themselves, Jay and Jarod hurried away from the reporters to speak with other hospital personnel. Approaching Jake, Sovic's nurse, they inquired of Sovic's visitors of late. The male nurse mentioned seeing a blond-haired guy with a crew cut wandering the hall near Sovic's room on the day of his death. It may be insignificant, but I didn't see anyone enter Sovic's room. I was very busy. If anyone tampered with his I.V., Sovic could have been overmedicated. Really, there is no way to know; things happen so fast around here. We can't be all eyes." Jake shrugged as if he was having a bad day.

"Do you guys think any untoward events could have occurred to worsen Sovic's condition? We're just trying to cover all bases in regard to his sudden death. He seemed to be improving the last time I visited," Chief Jared volunteered. "If you recall any questionable events, please contact us. We are trying to prevent mishaps while our prisoners are in custody."

"Sure, Chief Jarod, be sure to speak with Penny, Sovic's day nurse. She was in and out of his room often." Jake continued down the hall as he spoke.

"We'll definitely see her, Jake."

"She should be here tomorrow; today's her off day."

After surveying the surrounding area and questioning other personnel, Jay and Jared departed to the Herald office. Jay continued to brief Jared on other pertinent events of the day, while en route to the office.

Later that day Jay met Julie at the Coffee Shop. She seemed very happy that Kevin was home. She couldn't stop speaking of his time in the Cuban jail cell, and how he managed to get free with the aid of the Catholic church priest. And, that his mom was doing better.

"Jay, hope you meet your special someone soon, and know the joy I'm feeling today. You are such a sweet wholesome guy, you deserve the best." Julie remembered him sharing the break-up and despair he experienced with his former girlfriend. She had been 1nvolved in an auto accident shortly after he moved to Wyoming. He failed to mention details. He would just lower his head and grimace if she mentioned Rachel's name.

"Julie, I'm very happy for you, but you know you are my very best friend. Should anything come between you two, you know I'll be here to support you. I care a great deal for you. Be cautious with Kevin. You know his work involves danger. And, you realize what a close call he had with the plane mishap," Jay leaned closer and placed his hand upon hers.

"I'm aware, Jay. But, Kevin and I understand each other. He is a person of faith, as I am. And, that makes all the difference, believe me." Julie was quick to defend Kevin.

"Just remember, I'm here for you should you need me. We shall eventually capture all the persons involved in your kidnapping. Jarod has been progressively unraveling more information that could lead to more arrests of individuals who seem intent to cause chaos to our military maneuvers here and abroad. He is a determined investigator and won't stop until we see the hoodlums behind bars. They're a threat to us all with their underhanded sabotage tactics."

"Thanks, Jay. That is very reassuring." Julie was surprised at all Jay had revealed about his concern for her and all her friends and family.

He continued to brief her on the findings that

he and Jarod had gathered at the hospital. Jay then called Penny, Sovic's day nurse. And, yes, she did see a blond-haired guy holding onto the Russian's I.V. fluid bag.

"But I didn't notice anything irregular while I was in the room. Maybe I should've stayed a bit closer to the patient at that time." Jay thanked Penny and silenced his phone.

"No, Julie I didn't get the guy's name that Penny mentioned. But, do you think he could be the blond-haired person who bumped your car? You mentioned his blond hair."

"That is a possibility. Maybe Penny could identify him from some photos of suspicious characters the Feds are pursuing. I'd be willing to assist her if you think it would be helpful. We need to put away these guys."

"Julie, you sure are on top of all clues here. I'm glad you are on my team. We'll just notify Chief Jarod and he can get this 1nformation passed on to the Feds."

"If Penny could identify the blond-haired guy from some photos in the Feds. files, we might get a lead on who helped to create your accident." Jay grinned remembering Ms. Peterson's earlier suggestion. Julie arose to leave stating she must get home.

"Julie, I hate to see you go. We sure are covering some important issues. Please be careful. Don't take any changes as you drive to your moms. I'll keep going over all developments. If you remember anything else that might shed light on your kidnappers, or Sovic's death, give me a call-morning or night. I'll stay in touch. We'll get to the bottom of the leaks and consequences as soon as possible." Jay frowned to see Julie leave.

"Okay, Jay, I trust your judgement," Julie emphasized as she draped her coat over her shoulder, and tossed her hand through her flowing hair.

The next day came too soon for Julie and Kevin. Back at the hospital, Kevin's mom was already in the Cath. Lab. "Oh, Kevin, let's have a prayer for your mom while we wait. We can go to the chapel here on this floor. I spotted it on the way in." Inside the chapel were three other people. Julie later learned that they were also awaiting news of their family, and two were members of Kevin's family, Julie and Kevin embraced the couple and encouraged them to join them in prayer for Jackie, Kevin's mom. Holding hands with Kevin, Julie spoke first, and included verses from Psalms 121 1-2, NKJV:

> "Lord, be our comfort, shield, and protector at this hour as 'we look to the hills from whence cometh our help.' You are willing, Lord, and able to be with Jacqueline, at this very hour: to keep her strong. Also, enable the doctors and caregivers to obtain a diagnosis to aid in her treatment and recovery. Thank you

for providing for all our needs, Lord.
Amen."

Kevin then quoted the Lord's prayer with reverence
and devotion.

As they walked back to the waiting area, Kevin
spoke tenderly, "I have a peace about God's comfort,
Julie, from our prayers we uttered. My faith seems
uplifted and stronger in God."

An hour passed before Dr. Seay appeared at the
waiting room door. He approached, "Kevin, hello,
I have good news: your mom is doing fine, but she
does have some blockage. There is about a 50% in her
RCA. However, I do believe we can accomplish much
with the plans for her recovery and the up to date
medications of today. However, we must start her on
this regimen as soon as possible. She also appears
stronger than a few days earlier. She just needs
more rest at home, and then increase her activity
some each day."

"Thanks Dr. This is Julie Peterson, a close
friend of mine. We've both been worried about, Mom.
But, we feel confident she is receiving good care."

"Nice meeting you, Julie. We'll keep Mrs. Seals
through the night, but she should be able to return
home tomorrow if all goes well. We'll keep her
comfortable. Any questions?"

"No, thanks for the encouraging news, Doc."

"Stay in touch, Kevin." Dr. Seay smiled leaving
the room. Julie and Kevin went back to his mom's
room to await her return. Julie continued to talk
with Kevin about how long he could remain in town.

"Julie, I plan to stay a week if mom does

okay; then, it's back to Puerto Rico for further instructions. I hope to be back to the States in six months. I plan on us making some serious plans when I return. Will you wait for me, Julie?"

How could she resist those loving eyes, warm smile, and comforting voice.

"Of course, Kevin." Julie grasped his hand. "I feel as you do, that we've been busy the entire time you've been home. And, we have hardly had the opportunity to discuss us. Time is getting by too fast. I simply wish we could be together more."

"So do I, so do I, Julie. I do not intend to do these risky missions all of my life," Kevin was quick to assure Julie."

"I understand. Nor, do I wish to get involved in eerie events again. Although, God did see us through."

Two days later when Julie arrived home from work, Kevin had already arrived at Cecilia's house with a friend of his.

Meeting Julie at the door, he seemed eager to introduce his companion. "Julie, I want you to meet Jackie Evans. She is a great friend of my moms, and will be staying with her at times during the day when I'm on errands or busy in town."

"Hi, Jackie, nice to have you help Kevin at this needy time. I'm sure you shall be a help to Jacqueline, as well as, Kevin, since his leave from service is a short reprieve."

"Julie, if you have time later on, perhaps you could introduce Jackie to some of your friends. She mentioned that she would love to meet some new folks from around town since she's been away from home a few months. You know my mom would like for Jackie to be acquainted with a few more folks: she thinks her stay would be enhanced while here. My older sister, Kelly, from Utah, she plans to be here a few days. She and Jackie shall be with mom tonight while we're dining at the Hallebut."

"O Kevin, that sounds wonderful. Is your dad soon to return home from his sea excursion?" Julie questioned as they were preparing to leave.

"No, in fact, he is still on the Eisenhower out in the Gulf, as far as I know. You, realize some of his missions involve confidentiality. I'm sure mom will hear from him in a few days. She contacted Sam about her heart issues, but has not received any details as to his arrival date," Kevin embraced her waist as they said their goodbyes.

◄◄

While Kevin and Julie were at dinner, he mentioned how great Jackie would be with his mom. Listening with interest, Julie kept quiet wondering, *why hasn't he mentioned her before? She certainly didn't 'visit his mom in the hospital. Maybe I'm imagining things, but he sure has a keen knowledge of her. Well, I'm not going to draw-up the wrong conclusions.*

"Kevin, is Jackie employed at present, or just home some during the summer?" She didn't wish to be too intense or seem obvious, but she sure would like to feel free to learn more. Maybe, he wouldn't mind if she sent out feelers- if she was on vacation?

"No, she stays with her parents during the summer months, and teaches during the school season. She just seems lonely since she and her boyfriend, Jim broke up. Jim has moved to Texas with new employment," Kevin shrugged.

"Certainly, it would be nice if she and Jay could meet. I'll try to make it happen: maybe in church. I'll see what I can do." She smiled.

"Good luck, Julie. She doesn't seem to be pursuing anyone at present. But, who knows what shall develop with those two."

When Kevin kissed Julie goodnight, she hurried into her room with many questions. "How long shall Kevin's sister be at his moms? Would there ever be any guarantees in her work or relationships?"

Julie grabbed her Bible quickly after preparing for bed. Meditating on God's word, she read aloud Matthew 5:14-16, NKJV how... 'we are to be a light unto the world. A city upon a hill cannot be hid. We should let our light shine, so that all the world may see our good works, and glorify God.' She realized then, "I should be that shining light, not just to others, but to her family and friends." After much prayer, she determined she would try to abide, and get others to church Sunday. Now, closing her eyes for sleep, she had found some needed peace.

The next day after work, Julie met Kevin at his mom's for dinner. She was happy to see his mom up and about with more energy than she had noticed in the past few days. "Good to have you join us Julie," her mom was busy helping Kelly to prepare dinner.

Julie savored the aroma of ham as it wafted into the hallway. As Kevin and Jacqueline escorted her to the deck, she was again reminded of their great times together prior to Kevin's tour in Aguadilla, and terrible ordeal in Cuba. She had just rather dwell on the present, she decided for now. Too much discomfort to recall the last few weeks of their lives.

As Kevin's mom turned to go back inside, she whispered, "Julie, you two just enjoy the fresh air and my garden, while Kelly and I finish dinner. I have fresh tea." She hurried back through the French doors and brought them sparkling Russian tea.

"How refreshing," Julie exclaimed to Kevin. I may stay quite a while, if you're sure Jacqueline is up to all our tremendous appetites, "she grinned.

Kevin embraced her hand and said, "I'm planning on a lovely quiet evening with you close by, and if twilight comes upon us, the more romantic the atmosphere. I love moonlight strolls also, Julie," he tilted her face to gently kiss her.

After dinner, she had some pressing issues she wished to discuss with him.

As she and Kevin walked through the garden of lilies, roses, jasmine, and other spring flowers, the fragrance was nostalgic. Strolling down the lanes beyond the garden among the pines and crepe myrtles lining the narrow road, Kevin whispered how much she meant to him. Grasping her hand, he said, "I want to plan a life with you, Julie. I love you, and you are the center of my life. Of course God is number one in the universe. But here, today, if you feel as I do, I hope you will join me in a love fulfilled life with a closeness to God and family. I'm ready when I return from the service to prepare for a life with you."

"Julie, I plan to work with either a commercial or transport airline. I should be sending out some resumes for employment in the near future."

"O' Kevin, my heart is glad. I love you too. And, yes, I do share your feelings. My thoughts are definitely of endless time spent with you. I hope we can synchronize our work and living arrangements as we gain more in depth knowledge of how our work develops. I now have much confidence and faith in your abilities. I wish to be close to you," Julie turned and hugged Kevin with tenderness, feeling the rush of adrenaline and her accelerated heart thump.

"Thanks, Julie, I hope we can wed shortly after I return in August. We could live with my mom until we can purchase a home. Don't you agree?"

Julie rubbed her brow, "I know that may be a possibility, but let's wait and look at all of our options. Okay, Kevin?"

"That's probably a good idea, Julie"

I can see that Kevin is very serious. As they walked back to his mom's garden, he stopped to embrace. "I have never been happier," she responded as her heart tripped a few beats leaning against his warm muscular chest.

Gently, Kevin brushed her lips, then her neck. She responded capturing his lips with passion now knowing she could commit herself to him. She slowly released him with a hand to his face.

"I know that there will be many details of planning while you are away at the air base. I'll try to start work on some of those, Kevin." She shuttered to think of the next few months at work and not being able to see him. "I'm so relieved that you'll be out of the Air Force soon, and we can look to our future. He pulled from his pocket a small box. She gasped as he knelt and brought a ring out.

"Will you do me the honor of marrying me soon, Julie?" What could she say but, "Yesss, yes. It would be my utmost pleasure." He, then, placed the lovely diamond on her finger, and stood steadily to kiss her.

Back and into his mom's kitchen, Jacqueline mentioned a phone call for Kevin. "I couldn't recognize the voice, but I have the number written. The guy said it was urgent."

"Okay, Mom. I'll call after dinner. The aroma here is too great for me." With a warm savory rump roast with all the trimmings including cranberry sauce made with fresh fruit, mixed steamed vegetables with wild rice, and blueberry cobbler, the meal–who could delay the feast. After an humble prayer by Kevin, the meal began vanishing as they ravished the delectable entrees, as well as desserts.

Julie was anxious to know about Kevin's call, and was about to question him, when he arose from the table, excusing himself, to answer the phone call.

Returning, he stated, "It was Colonel O'Neal, Mom. And Julie, he needs me to report back to Aguadilla as soon as possible. He said the President had extra missions in store."

"I know it's a new assignment, or he would not have interrupted my leave this soon. I'll have to head out early in the morning." Kevin clasped Julie's hands and held them. I'll see you safely home. As they headed back, Julie mentioned, that she would be moving back to her apartment. "I'll not leave mom's until I'm sure it's safe," she confided.

"Please don't move back home until all the villains connected with your accident and kidnapping are behind bars," Kevin urged. I would stay worried for your safety otherwise."

"Yes, I must speak with Jay and Jarod to be sure all their criminal surveillance has been met with successful undertaking... And I'm getting a dog, Kevin. It will be, for all intent, a watch-dog: one that won't just whimper at the sound of a silent intruder!"

"Good, that makes me feel better already, Julie," Kevin exclaimed, embracing her waist.

"Stepping out onto the veranda, out of nowhere came, "Is Jackie still staying at your mom's house these days?"

"Not now that mom is stronger; she just checks in on her from time to time."

Giving a sigh of relief, Julie volunteered, "Can I help her in any way, Kevin? Does she need transportation to and from the doctor?"

"No, she doesn't go that often, and my sister shall be here for two more weeks. She is fine now. Maybe later, she might need a helping hand." Kevin began revealing to Julie about his duties and again suggesting that she and her church pray daily. And that he would be on assignment in a couple of days. "Don't you worry, I've been trained for all flight maneuvers" he replied as he kissed her goodnight, and headed out the door. She stood at the door and waved good-bye. He had looked her way; then turned, and entered his vehicle.

Julie guessed it was serious missions for Kevin as soon as she heard him mention his duty to his country. She suddenly took her cell phone and dialed his number. When he answered the call, she said, "I won't question you, Kevin, but please be careful. And I shall be in prayer with my family for your safety and accomplishments each day. Let me know when Series #1 is over."

"I'll call you as often as I can. I love you, Julie. Wait for me," Kevin pleaded.

"You're part of my life now, Kevin. I won't think of anything else but your safe return." As Julie silenced her cell, she stopped to pray. *God, we need your blessings, and guidance on all on-going activities with the U.S. military. Efforts to retain peace and security in our nation, is of utmost importance.*

After her prayer, she went immediately to notify her mom for more prayer support.

FOURTEEN

Back at the Herald, Julie and Jay had learned that the guy who bumped her car was definitely involved in her kidnapping, and that he had visited Sovic in the hospital. "We must assist the Federal authorities with locating this guy," Julie insisted to Jay.

Jarod appeared without notice, and overhearing Julie, he scowled at them, "Guys, please leave everything up to the Feds. It is just too dangerous for you two to get involved in this investigation. You must realize that we are probably dealing with a killer. Neither of you should submit yourselves to this danger."

"I'll assure you, Jarod, that we have more assignments than we can take care of these days. But, if we come near any unusual happenings or leads..., I'll be the first to call you. By the way, have the Feds. had any answers to queries on Lt. Caleb? You know, he turned over classified files to Julie. It would be interesting to know all of his connections with others involved in these investigations" Jay questioned.

"No, not that I'm aware of, but I'll gather as many facts as I can from the authorities and Seth

Faust at the U.S. Department of Defense. Lieutenant Brown did communicate with Faust: he should be able to give us some insight into this scenario," Jarod was quick to assure Jay.

Julie waited until Jarod left the Herald building to inform Jay how she felt. "I can hardly believe this guy that did these acts of violence would be such a dare-devil to still be around. He must be getting compensated very well. I'd like to see him arrested. He'll need to be behind bars before I feel safe again. Jay, will you escort me to my mom's today? I haven't moved back to my apartment yet. And, I don't plan to give this fellow a chance to step on my toes again. I'd also like to be confident that my mom is not involved in any extraneous situations."

"Julie, I told you that I'd be here for you as much as you need me. And, I'll be happy to escort you to your moms." Jay reassured her. "Try to stay calm. We'll get these thugs soon. They can't keep evading the authorities, The investigators have them pegged, and they're just waiting for more movement."

―◄━

As Julie entered her office the next day, she was met by Jerome. "Julie have you heard the latest news today about the Cuban Crisis? It seems our President is applying more pressure on Russia to assist with the elimination of the missile build-up in Cuba."

"No, Jerome, I didn't get the news this morning. How can we help here at the Herald?"

"Phil Connor is out today, but he left word that he would like for you to report to Washington today, if possible and obtain all the details that can be gathered on the President, and the Defense Department's plan for resolving the Missile Crisis with Cuba."

"We need you to get updates for at least one week in Washington for the Herald, Ms. Julie. Then, Jay can follow-up the next week, while you return to your present assignment.

"Jerome, I would be honored to get this assignment, but I need to leave immediately to obtain tickets. I'm not sure about a flight out today. I would need to purchase a few items for the trip. Can Jay cover my present assignment until I return? He's become familiar with the area, and I could render him my research on the case."

"Sure, Julie, I've checked, and there is a flight out by American Airlines this afternoon to Washington. If you could get those needed items pronto here in town, and be ready, then, you need to be on the plane!"

◄◄

Julie made haste to leave the office, and prepare for her flight. Calling Jerome from her vehicle, she reminded Jerome that she may need an escort in Washington since she still had unresolved issues with her kidnappers, and she wasn't familiar with the area near the capitol. "I need someone to direct me to the President's briefings, and to any meetings with the Press."

"Julie, I've already contacted one of the Washington journalist, Callie Severence, to meet-up with you at the airport. She is to assist you with contacts, and data gathering. Also, she is good friend of mine, and is knowledgeable of the area; someone who knows the inner circle of the White House, and the press," Jerome confided.

"O' great, Jerome, I really appreciate you taking care that I don't have shortcomings. Perhaps Callie can also assist Jay when he arrives here next week."

"Exactly, Julie. Keep your chin up. Everything should be fine. No one should know of your assignment except me, Jay, and Phil. Make your reports out to Jay, and he should be updated on all happenings prior to our publications. We shall be delighted to get some news-worthy columns soon, Julie. Your news-gathering should capture the headlines!

"I'll gladly comply. And, Jay can keep me updated on my former assignment here at the Herald. Thanks, Jerome," Julie replied as she headed out to prepare for her next journey.

◄━

As Julie was arriving at the airport, her phone rang. "Speaking. Hi Kevin, great to hear from you. I'm off to begin an assignment in Washington D.C. How are things developing in Aguadilla? I'm missing you terribly."

"I'll be leaving tomorrow on Series One of my flights. I'm not able to reveal any details, but I may be out of the country for a few days. President Kennedy definitely has a new agenda. Everything is classified. He and Bobby (his brother) are having some secret back-channel communications with Krushchev. Even after Krushchev posted in a letter to our President that our military blockade would be a act of aggression, he is still strongly threatening what could materialize into a nuclear missile war."

"Julie, the U.S. is on the brink of war if our blockade backfires. Please be in prayer tonight, and have the church warriors continue in prayer daily," Kevin pleaded before he bade her good-bye.

Julie met Callie almost as soon as she stepped off of the plane. *My, she is a stunning-looking petite reporter. And, she sure seems to know her way around, and will certainly be a good mentor,* Julie considered.

Callie directed Julie to the Hilton Hotel. "Your room is next door to mine. I hope that agrees with you, Julie?"

"I feel safer and more comfortable with you close by, Callie. Now, I can concentrate on the daily events taking place here in Washington. I'll probably be able to get news out faster in this setting in close proximity to the White House, and I'm looking forward to being a part of those who hear the news first-hand; then, get it out to others."

Daybreak came too soon the next day. After a breakfast of fruit parfait, cheese, croissants, and oatmeal, Julie and Callie headed out for an early press meeting at the White House.

"Wow, I'm not privileged to such a large breakfast," Julie exclaimed.

"You'll certainly need it for the lengthy press

conference we're attending. It will probably last until twelve noon, and the press interaction is intense. Be prepared with your questions. And, don't be hesitant to ask specifics, if you need some details for your newspaper. After all, that's how we learn, and keep our President alert for other options to follow or review-for his decision-making endeavors in times of crisis. We're an important resource for his brain-storming too."

Upon arriving at the conference, Julie reviewed her series of inquiries which included: Kennedy's negotiations with Krushchev, the prospects of possible war, the U.S.'s bargaining ideas with Cuba, etc. "I hope to gain more insight into where Kennedy stands on our strategic plans with Cuba and Russia at this crucial stage of his private interactions," Julie confided to Callie.

Callie is correct on the time frame of these meetings. My morning has been well spent on news gathering. I am expanding my view, and see the importance of being here to recognize how every piece of the puzzle must fall into place. Julie listened closely. Of course, that is what the President is hoping; he can fulfill his contingency plans.

"O' Callie, how we need to pray. I must call mom this afternoon. I'm concerned about my friend, Kevin. Will he be detained in the Air Force if the Crisis is not resolved?"

Arriving back at her hotel, Julie promptly called her mom. "Mom, I need to know what you and Kevin's mom and dad think about this on-going Cuban situation. Do you think the U.S. can resolve this in a timely manner."

"Well, we've discussed it fervently. Much is going to depend on the convincing of Russia of intent. And you must realize we are praying each day for peace. I'm sure that you know, as well as I, that both Russia and Cuba want to be win as players. The President shall have to come up with a plan that is a gain-gain for all parties in this vexed triangle. If he can do that, and prevent a conflict, we are on the way to peace. The U.N. may have to be involved in the resolution."

"We shall surely be in prayer, and so will our church folks be on their knees during these trying days. I am indeed hoping that the Catholics in Cuba are about their prayers also," Cecilia exclaimed.

"Mom, if I speak with Kevin by phone, I'll discuss our plans for prayer partners, and how we might help with the peace initiative back home. I can't say enough about how we must support our military, and involve everyone we know who might lend an ear to how we can save lives. We must prevent this impending war with the muscle we know our American citizens can contribute. To halt the Russians and Cubans in their build-up of weapons of mass destruction, is our primary goal at present."

"Julie, I'm with you all the way with this on-going crisis intervention. Let me know when you hear word from Kevin about the latest developments at the base in Aguadilla. I'll speak with our church leaders again and try to get them prepared for all aspects of prayer and contributions to help our military. We need every person who has a heart for our country to help."

Upon returning to Aguadilla, Kevin met with

Colonel O'Neal shortly after his arrival. After saluting and greeting the Colonel, O'Neal was quick to get down to business. "Lieutenant Seals, good to see you. As I spoke with you by phone, the President is getting our Air Force ready with all expediency. Your first mission is up-coming. Are you prepared to take to the skies again?"

"Yes, Sir. I was expecting an 'all hands on deck' approach to our service, since Krushchev is testing the ability of our President."

"Right, your first assignment starts in two days. Kevin, you shall meet Lt. Commander Darwick Lewis at the Army Garrison, Vicenza, Italy, on May 25. The garrison is located one mile from Ghedin in Northern Italy. Your cargo will be stored at the airbase there. It should be ready at a moment's notice should the U.S. need to respond quickly to Russian threats from the events brewing in Cuba."

"As you return on May 27th, be ready for a flight to Turkey with similar cargo that you transported to Italy. We must be ready to go, when, and if, our President gives the go-ahead. We are not bluffing our way out of this. We're preparing ourselves. Since your plane is carrying military defensive armament, you shall have other planes, equipped, who will accompany you.

CHAPTER
FIFTEEN

Calling Julie, Kevin unloaded his new assignments.

"Series #1 of my missions shall take place immediately, Julie. And #2 shall follow as soon as I return to Aguadilla. As you know all is classified and I'm unable to give you any specifics. So, just trust and pray."

"Kevin, stay focused, and know that I shall stay in prayer for you and your comrades. I'm on assignment, and I have learned a great deal from the President's press conference today. You shall surely be briefed when you return to Ramey Air Base in Puerto Rico," Julie exclaimed.

"Julie, I love you, and keep check on mom for me.. Yes, I'll call as soon as I return to Aguadilla. I'm hopeful that I'll be home soon."

Back at the Herald, Jay received a call. "Jay, when shall Julie be back to work? I need to speak with her," the caller replied.

"Who's calling?" Jay questioned.

"Just tell her it's her friend from work at the Western Herald. She'll know who I am."

Not recognizing the voice, Jay commented, "Maybe I could help. She is on assignment at present. She should be in this week-end, but I'm not sure."

"I'll look for her at her mom's this week end," the caller relayed to Jay, silencing his phone.

How did this guy know Julie would be at her mom's, Jay puzzled. Jay immediately called Julie's mom, Cecilia.

◄◄

"I have no idea who might be calling," Cecilia stated, answering Jay's call. I have not heard Julie mention anyone at the Herald that she might consider contacting her. I think we should be on guard about this individual, Jay. I'll get in touch with Julie and inquire about this issue. I am frankly frightened to think someone would be coming here to meet-up with my daughter."

"Okay, Cecilia, please don't allow anyone to visit that you don't anticipate, or know personally; don't answer the door if they don't call first and give you a familiar name."

"You can be sure of that, Jay," Cecilia replied, silencing her phone.

Well, I'll have to meet Julie's plane and escort her, Jay realized. He called Chief Jarod who immediately started to prepare police protection for Julie's arrival back home.

Jay was uneasy about the caller. He began inquiring at the Herald as to who had heard from

Julie, pretending he had not heard from her. None the less, no one seemed to know of her whereabouts. Surich, her friend, mentioned she assumed Julie was on leave for a few days. Jay promised Surich he'd try to reach her tonight.

As Jay drove home from work, he couldn't get his mind off the caller. Why hadn't he given him his name. Upon arriving home, Jay rushed into his house. Locating Julie's number, he dialed the Hilton in Washington. Julie answered promptly.

◄◄

"Hello Jay, I was about to call your house and give you my report from the President's press conference."

"Julie, someone called me today wanting to know your location. It was not Kevin. I didn't recognize the voice.

The party stated you'd know; that they were a friend of yours from the Herald." Jay assured her.

"Jay I have no idea who it could've been."

"Listen, Julie, you'll just need to be very careful. I'll meet you at the airport, and I'll notify your mom not to go to the door unless she sees us, or my vehicle pull into the drive way. Not alarming you, but it may be an unwanted visitor."

Now Julie was uneasy. She had felt safe in Washington, but, now... What if it was the blond-haired guy who had bumped my vehicle. *I'll be ready for him, if it is indeed him! Jay and Jarod would see to that event,* she was sure.

Julie checked all her doors at the Hilton: all

doors locked. She then called Callie. "Callie, stay with me at all times tomorrow. An unknown caller phoned Jay at the Herald today. Jay said he sounded suspicious. No, he didn't leave his name, but stated he was a friend of mine; that, I don't believe. The guy said he would meet me when I arrived home. Can you believe that?"

"Yes, Julie, you can't be too careful these days with this Cuban situation brewing. I'll be there for you tomorrow. It should be safe here. We'll have security at the meetings. Call if you need anything, night or day." Callie cautioned her.

"Callie, I'll have a special prayer tonight for you, myself, and our families. I'm not adept of all things that can go wrong in this precarious situation that I am a part of. But, my kidnapping wasn't just a fluke; those guys were out to get information from me. I just happened to be very vulnerable because I did not realize what game players in foreign government could pull off.

My files that I had obtained secretly would be a risk to my life. I'm ready for more protection from now on instead of risking my safety needlessly.

"Yes, Julie, use all caution from heretofore to avoid foul play in our country."

As night was upon her, Julie read her Bible. The chapters capturing her attention were from Psalms #:3-4, revealing how God was all powerful and protective of his own. Comparing herself to David, how he cried out to God for his love and protection: now she was crying out for herself, friends, family, and country, and others involved in this Cuban Crisis.

She finished her reading with a sense of peace for the moment as she closed the book with a word of prayer.

◄◄

"Lieutenant Kevin, are you ready for #2 mission tomorrow?" Colonel O'Neal questioned him as he returned to the air base.

"Yes, Sir." I've gone through the exercises and flight plan several times, and I believe the weather should be favorable, Sir."

"You know the President has again called our attention to his crucial negotiations with Krushchev. He reiterated the necessity of our readiness at all times in the event Moscow doesn't pull back on missile build-up in Cuba. Ramey officials assured him we are indeed preparing for whatever the situation warrants, Lieutenant. We are relying upon you to lead this second mission," Colonel O'Neal informed him. "And, I have all confidence that we'll be ready to maneuver our team as needed."

"Then, I'll leave out early a.m., Sir. Our pilots are ready and willing to keep our country secure, rest assured."

Kevin called Julie. Unable to reach her, he left her a message of the his flight plan: ending the call with, "I love you, Julie."

◄◄

The next morning Julie could not believe she'd missed his call. As she checked her phone, finding his lovely message, she murmured to herself, "It's too late to call back. He's probably in flight by now."

Callie met Julie in the dining area. "Let's prepare for more news briefs."

Julie answered by bowing her head in prayer-"for more protection, strength, and knowledge in all endeavors to do my job. Protect Kevin with direction, and skill to carry out his mission. Be with my family, Lord, and all those involved in the peace process for our nation. Everything I ask, Lord, is in your name: for your glory. Amen." She uttered with devotion.

Callie commented, as deeply moved, "I am thankful for your leadership in prayers for us, Julie. I must start following your example more, and calling upon God. He must have the answers to all our needs."

As they departed the hotel for the press conference, Julie voiced, "I'm more at peace knowing God is near."

Upon arriving at the White House, they were promptly briefed by the President's Press Secretary on the serious events of the Cuban military build-up. As Julie listened, her mind wandered to the phone call Jay had received yesterday... Who at the Herald needed to meet her at her mom's? Remembering Finlay, and possibly Sayvinsky; would they risk an encounter with me knowing their present scrutiny by the Feds? *I hope not.*

"Callie, I'm thankful Jay has obtained a gun for me, even if I haven't learned to use it. Of course, I had a little practice session with Jay and Jarod at the firing range a few weeks ago, but that was not nearly enough to sustain accuracy," Julie murmured.

Callie quickly questioned her, but Julie just sighed, "I don't wish to alarm you, there are just serious events in our country: we need to be prepared," she said quietly.

◄◄

Friday came sooner than Julie anticipated. As she boarded her plane for Topeka, she was thankful for her first-hand knowledge from the President and his staff: the details of the Cuban Crisis. Phil Connor will be happy to get the news headlines published in the Herald by this week-end, she smiled knowingly. She managed to doze some during the flight as fatigue overcame her.

As the stewardess called out, "fasten your seat-belts for descent into Topeka," Julie aroused from her nap. The flight had seemed less burdensome this time.

◄◄

Jay was smiling and waving as Julie arrived at the terminal. "Jay, is it safe to return to mom's?"

Yes, Julie, we have security personnel and vans at your mom's house. If anyone tries anything, we'll be there to protect you."

"I think I'll just stop by and check on Kevin's mom first, if you don't mind, Jay?"

Sure, Julie, I'll brief Jarod. He's probably at your mom, Cecilia, by now."

When Jay spoke with Chief Jarod, he informed him that two vans had passed them. They could possibly be en route to Julie's mom," Jay suggested. "Is Detective Seville with you?"

"Yes, Jay, he'll monitor the house. You know the vans that you saw could be beyond the sycamores that line Cecilia's fence, about one-half mile down the road. I'm going to circle around back, through the woods, and see if I can get a lead on the situation. I'll take my K-9 dog with me."

"Jarod, please be careful. Julie and I should be there in about fifteen minutes. Please don't put yourself in any danger. We're stopping by Kevin's mom's on the way over."

"That's fine, Jay. I have an officer with Cecilia now. That should be more security for her and Julie, once Julie arrives. And she, Cecilia, is aware of all the circumstances, and she shall be on alert. We're not taking any chances that these guys are not armed. We are well equipped to meet the challenge if these guys wish to play hard-ball. I'll keep my men on surveillance updated as to any unusual developments in the area. We're familiar with the area, and it's a peaceful community; we wish to sustain it."

After checking on Kevin's mom, Jacqueline, and assuring. She was recuperating well, both Julie and Jay departed for Cecilia's. "I'm happy I was able to finally meet Jackie Evans, Jacqueline's caregiver and neighbor," Jay volunteered.

"Yes, she seems very caring and dedicated to her.

I'm sorry we were unable to stay longer, but we need to hurry on home, since we're expected by Jarod. And, who knows what awaits?" Julie cried.

As Jay drove on, he commented, "Jackie is a lovely lady, and seems to be a caring person," he smiled, trying to distract Julie.

"Yes, I believe she's unattached too, Jay. She's just here for the summer. Maybe you and she could get to know each other better."

"When I return from Washington next week, we'll see."

As they reached Cecilia's house, Jay's phone dinged. Answering the call, he heard, "Jay, I saw only one van near the lake behind Cecilia's house. I'm using binoculars, and it looks as if two people occupy the van," Jared mentioned. "I don't think they have spotted me. When you get Julie inside the house, come around the back of the house, and meet me on the path near the sycamores. But crouch down, I can't determine yet if they're· scouring the house, are if they're about to depart and approach the lake. We'll see what these two suspicious characters are nosing about. They seemed preoccupied, but I'll soon garner their weapons, I'll almost promise you. And, Jay, notify Detective Seville, and the officer inside the house of the two snoops near the lake; 'our objective to take out, if need be.'" Jarod didn't skip a beat delivering his instructions, and keeping his men posted of their surveillance.

Jay hurriedly escorted Julie into her mom's house, and notified Detective Seville, and the other officer. With his Glock, and protective vest in place, he raced to meet Chief Jarod.

"Chief, this is almost like old times when I worked with you. I hope we get these dudes, if they're the ones conniving against Julie."

"Let's don't make this a habit, Jay, even though I did temporarily deputize you. You don't need to jeopardize your safety. If we meet resistance, I have back-up near the inter section up ahead. I don't think these..." Jay interrupted as they neared the vehicle.

"One of the guys is Bill Finlay, and the other.. he has blonde hair. Where do you think the other van disappeared to?"

"Regardless, I'm calling for back-up," Jarod whispered cautiously. "I'm not sure that the other van is involved.

"I don't think these guys will risk foul play with a police presence in the vicinity. However, they may not realize that some of the officers are in unmarked vehicles. We won't take any chances with Julie being a culprit."

"Look, Jarod! One of them is getting out of his vehicle. Shall we close in?" Jay suggested.

"No, let's see what... it looks like Finlay- is up to, Jay. Surely he is not going back to Cecilia's house." Jarod quickly phoned Officer Sam Little on the other side of the lake. "Sam, one of the suspects is on foot. He may be headed back in your direction. He has dark-cropped hair, and is dark-skinned."

"I'll be ready for him if he migrates this way, Chief."

A few minutes later, Julie heard glass break

near the kitchen door. She hurried to call Sgt. Pino, who was with her mom in the living room. Pino rushed to the back door to find Finlay- trying to break in. Sergeant called, "halt" as the door was opening. Turning, the assailant, glared at the gun, and attempted to flee, but Pino was quick to pursue.

Julie soon heard shots ring out, and looked out the window to see Pino grab his left arm. "Pino was hit, and the assailant managed to disappear into the woods behind Cecilia's barn," Julie cried out. With heart racing, she ran to check on her mom.

"I'm sure I wounded him," Officer Pino exclaimed, as he returned to the kitchen door. "There's a blood trail near the barn. Pino quickly called Officer Little, "Finlay has fled. He's wounded." Acknowledging the call, Little called an ambulance and notified Chief Jarod.

"Yes, Sam, we see Finlay headed back to his van, and we're in pursuit from the lake area. Jarod phoned Officer Pino again, but, - silenced his phone, and yelled, "halt." Shots were fired as Finlay fiercely struggled to reach his van. He managed to jump into the van, and the van sped off. Chief Jarod fired his Glock at the vehicle, hitting one of the tires. He radioed ahead. The officer at the intersection noted a van speeding in his direction with a wobble in one of his tires. A police chase ensued.

Shortly thereafter, the van was stopped by the two officers who had been in pursuit. Both suspects were arrested. Finlay was soon transported to the county hospital with a leg wound.

Jay and Chief Jarod breathed a sigh of relief that Sergeant Pino was the only officer wounded.

Julie had wrapped both his left arm and shoulder in bandages. The ambulance was soon to transport him to the West-End Hospital. Finley, they learned, was now undergoing surgery in the county hospital. He was also in protective custody.

"Julie, I know you're relieved to hear that both men in the van have been captured. Now, maybe you'll have relief from some fear, and anxiety. Both were either directly or indirectly involved in the plot to obtain the Witherton Files," Jay said.

"I hope this is the end of your headache and stress,"

Cecilia hugged her daughter as she tried to reassure her.

"Yes, Mom, I think we are turning corners in solving my car accident, and kidnapping from the hospital. Now, if Kevin can fulfill his obligations to the military, both his and my family can hope for a more secure future."

"Mom, I would like to invite Jay, Jackie, and Kevin's mom to church Sunday. We need to sow seeds of kindness and love today; especially, since we see the Crisis in Cuba, and our nation's involvement. There is too much uncertainty among the U.S., Cuba, and Russia. Don't - you think that's a good idea, Mom? Besides, we need more prayer warriors for our military," Julie exclaimed.

Cecilia was quick to agree. "And, perhaps we can solicit the help of the Pope to pray for all countries involved in the plans for negotiations by our leaders. Let's reach out to others, Cecilia said. I've heard it said that God is ever near unto us, if we pray and trust in His word. I believe the Pope could have an impact on our countries reaching a peaceful resolution to these conflicts. Let's have faith and prayer."

"Mom, I'll write Kevin another letter to send to his Command Center. It should enlighten him to our prayer efforts. He should receive it when he returns to his base. I'll be sure he's aware that we're backing him and his men one hundred per cent. They must realize all encouragement from us and our country."

CHAPTER
SIXTEEN

Kevin's second mission was underway to Turkey when he received a call from Colonel O'Neal. "Lieutenant Kevin, the President is requesting we expedite the completion of our flight missions as soon as possible. Tensions are building with Fidel and Kruschev. We think the sea and air blockade(Code name: Quarantine)is going to be successful. We just want to be ready to move if other decisive measures are needed. I shall send two more teams to support and beef-up security with your cargo delivery, and other elements. I can't say enough about how we are depending on you and your team. Even if you are not the Rainbow Squad, you are more thorough in your mission accomplishments, Lieutenant.

Not familiar with the Rainbow Squad, Kevin had heard rumors of an elite group of individuals that only answered to the President. "Well, when I return to Ramey Air Base, I'll have to research this a little more, and just see if we compare. We only answer to your orders, Sir. But, as I must always strive to improve my performance, I'll seek to remember to be adept," Kevin promised.

"Thanks, Colonel, we'll continue with the process

as you've directed. Keep us posted on any new developments as we press on. We should be returning to Ramey Air Base soon for our further instructions." Kevin and the team kept up the mission with precision and focus. There'd been only one incident with a malfunction of one of the carrier's landing gear: not tragic. Lieutenant Jerry Volter simply didn't have any choice but to abort one of his flights, and double his efforts for a safe landing on his second approach. All ground crew were using all skill to help get the plane safely landed. It took tremendous ability by the pilot to get the landing gear positioned properly for a smooth landing.

On the third month of Kevin's enlistment, Julie received word from him that most of his overseas missions were completed. "I hope to get a leave to visit you and Mom soon. Then, my discharge should soon be in the picture," he wrote. "I'm long overdue to be with you, and reassure you that the long wait for us is just about over. If President Kennedy can help end this Crisis we're in, I should get out as scheduled. Otherwise, I may get detained a while longer. Just pray for me daily, Julie."

"I'm indeed praying, and so is my prayer group at church." Julie continued her letter. "*Kevin I am also scouting" the neighborhood for a place for us to reside in hopes that you can find employment close by. If not we shall decide other options when you return. You'll be happy to hear Kevin, that Chief Jarod, Jay, and other officers helped to capture one of my kidnappers. Do you remember Jim Fray? He was the guy that bumped my car when I had the auto ac ident. Also Bill Finlay was helping the thugs and was arrested.*

Prayers are being answered. I am still looking to God each day the author and finisher of our faith.

Julie closed the letter with, *Love, Julie.*

Here it is September 1962, and I'm off to Washington to continue Julie's press meetings. This is most generous of President Kennedy to finally allow us to meet with him at the White House. I can't recall any other President being this open and inviting with the Press. Getting the latest updates on the Cuban Crisis, Jay wrote:

> The latest news is that Krushchev is feeling the pressure applied by President Kennedy to get the missiles removed from Cuba. The word around Washington is that Krushchev and Kennedy are having secret back-channel communications to initiate an end to the Crisis.
>
> I have also heard from other reporters that Pope John's prayers may be having an effect. They say that he has influenced Krushchev about the 'doomsday' potential from a nuclear holocaust if peace is breached.

Julie was elated to read all of Jay's report for the Herald. Seems he's getting better news than I. I hope all this means the U.S. is about to resolve the missile issue with Cuba. Kevin could be coming home soon! "Hurray, hurray," Julie could be heard cheering from her office.

After Jay returned to Kansas on Friday, he met Julie at the Herald office with a big smile. "I have great vibes about our President, Julie. My anticipations for his success with negotiations have increased since I had a chance to meet him. I believe we'll hear some good news soon. I heard he is to meet with the U.N. on Monday."

October came in with a bang, everyone was up-in-the-air about the evening news. T.V. anchors were announcing:

> October, 1962, with the aid of the United Nations, Sec. Gen. Uthant, President Kennedy, and Premier Krushchev reached a peaceful agreement (mainly to remove missiles from Cuba per Russia, and for the U.S. to remove those missiles in Turkey and Italy with U.N. confirmation on both sides.) And, there is not to be an invasion of Cuba by the U.S.

"I am so happy to hear the great news. Maybe Kevin and I can begin our marriage plans," Julie almost shouted.

"Yes, Julie, things are looking up. Do you think we might have lunch together now that Kevin may be coming home soon, and the villains are out of circulation?" Jay asked.

"I think that is a definite, yes. Allow me to

call Mom, and tell her our plans: she's expecting me home early."

"I'll come by your desk at noon and we'll visit the nearby deli," Jay answered with a winning grin.

"That should be fine," Julie spoke, listening to her mom's conversation on her phone.

At lunch, Jay discussed more of the President's quotes from his Washington press conference. "It seems the Crisis will be resolved soon, Julie. How is Kevin doing?"

"He's fine and coming home soon, I'm sure. I am thrilled we can start future plans together," her elation shining through those large dark eyes.

"I'm happy for you, Julie, if that is what you're convinced is best. But, remember what I said, that I care deeply for you and your safety. If you need me, I'll be close by. I'm not going away." Although, I'm now friends with Jackie Evans, she'll be back teaching soon. She is a great lady, and I hope we can stay in touch. But, distance makes a relationship a little strained."

"Jay, I'll pray for you, your family, and Jackie daily. I'll forever be your friend. I'd probably not be alive if you and Jarod had not been here. Thanks for giving me another chance at life." Julie teared-up as she spoke. "Let's not get so involved in our work that we forget all safety rules. And, I'll try not to be as vulnerable again. We're young, and there should be much awaiting us in our future," she confessed.

"That goes for me also, Julie. I'll try to be paired with another person in risky situations in the future. Our next assignment involves traveling to Alaska in search of a missing cruise ship. We may recruit two more people to travel with us for better security." Jay commented.

"That's a must for me from my prospective," Julie replied. "Let's all celebrate when Kevin returns, and always support one another in faith, work, and family. That's my wish for our future," Julie confessed.

CHAPTER
SEVENTEEN

As Julie was driving home from work, trying to forget her words with Jay, her phone binged. Quickly answering the call, she greeted, "Hello, Kevin. Yes, I'm headed home, and happy to retire from an eventful day. Are you nearby? I'm hoping for a restful afternoon."

"Julie, I have good news. I just received a letter from the American Airlines informing me that I've been selected to be employed as an interim pilot at Forbes Air Base."

"Great, Kevin, that sounds wonderful. Will you get to begin soon?"

"Wait, there's more. Also, I'll have a full-time position in two months as pilot for their transcontinental flights to Europe." Speaking with excitement, he continued, "You know what this means for our future. It will enable us to live near Topeka, and close to our parents. Wouldn't that be swell?"

Kevin, I'm very happy for you. Does that mean we can start to celebrate the good news tonight? And, maybe wine and dine together?"

"Indeed, Julie, and I know just the place; it is only a one hour drive from here. The food is fantastic. Shall we say seven p.m. tonight?"

"That should be fine," Julie exclaimed. We can start plans for our future, Kevin! I'm anxious to hear all the other details that you heard today. I'll see you at Mom's at seven, then," she commented before she hurried on home.

◄◄

After a dinner of prime rib, luscious mixed vegetables, rice pilaf, wine, etc., Julie's generous smile and warmth to Kevin's touch, spoke volumes to him. "I plan to take a few days off to talk with realtors, and we can also look at some houses, if that is agreeable with you, Kevin?"

"Yes, and our wedding plans can accelerate. I have a few more details to attend to," he grinned as he mentioned rings, the church, etc. They both had agreed on the Catholic church for the wedding venue. "But, I predict it may take one or two months to get settled in my work, housing, etc."

"God has been good, Kevin. We just need to stay close to Him at all times, especially, since we've both had daring events in our lives the last few months."

Julie was about to discuss her work assignment with Kevin, when she looked up to see- none other than Surich Placusky. "Hello," she greeted. Surich nodded. "Surich, I'd like for you to meet my fiance, Kevin Seals. Kevin, this is a friend of mine from the Herald, Ms. Surich Placusky." Kevin said his hello, and motioned for her to be seated with them. After their greetings and acknowledgements, Surich mentioned, "I need a few minutes with you in private, Julie."

Julie excused herself, and they went to a private area near the entrance of the restaurant.

Surich immediately scowled at Julie. "Why did you tell Jay that I would be suitable for the Alaskan assignment? Sure I lived there, but I have good reasons not to return. I was escaping a bad relationship when I came to Topeka. I have no desire to return. You must realize that you're the best qualified for the trip. I'm not about to risk my safety on another endeavor in that area."

"Okay, okay, Surich! I had no idea you had these issues. I'll see if Kevin and I can work together on our plans. Maybe, I'll be able to go with the team. I really need this time with him. But, if we can solve some of our housing and marital plans e-early..." She stuttered. "I hope we can survive my being in Alaska two or three weeks," Julie lowered her head as she spoke softly.

"I'll help you any way that I can, Julie. I have some contacts with some realtors in this area, and I can probably come up with a rental property that would be great, or, if you prefer to buy a starter home.."

"No, we prefer to rent for a few months until Kevin's work is well established." Julie was quick to recommend."

"I'll get right on it, Ms. Julie," Surich assured her as she was departing. "Tell, Kevin, nice to meet him," she voiced, as she said her goodbye near the restaurant door.

Kevin was all ears when Julie returned. "What was that all about, Julie?"

"It just concerned our work schedule. "I'll tell

you more when we get home. Mom was not feeling well when I left home; I need to check on her."

———◀━

When they arrived at Julie's mom's, Julie hurried on into Cecilia's bedroom; Kevin lingered beside the bedroom door. "Mom, are you feeling better?" she inquired as she approached her bedside.

Arousing easily, Cecilia said, "Yes, I'm fine, Julie. My headache is subsiding. Since I ate and had Advil, I'm much better. Did you and Kevin have a nice dinner celebration?"

"Of course, Mom, Kevin is here." She motioned him in.

"We were a little interrupted by my co-worker, Surich. I know you've heard me mention her, the redhead from Alaska. It seems she's unable to go on the Alaskan assignment. How am I going to manage this and my wedding, Mom? Please tell me."

Julie turned to hear Kevin gasp. "Kevin, I'm sorry to break this news to you, but we can discuss this more later."

Kevin's eyebrows raised and Julie could see the flushing of his face. "I'm sure we'll check into this situation. We'll deal with it, Mrs. Peterson. Don't you worry," Kevin reassured.

"Mom, if I can get many of our wedding and housing plans taken care of, I think Kevin would be more receptive for me to be away a few days. Surich also agreed to assist me with locating a house," Julie asserted.

"I'm here for you, Julie. I can help with your

wedding dress, and plans. I know a wonderful catering service nearby for the reception: food, drinks, etc. We've already discussed the attendants, guest list; and the church will be lovely adorned by the wedding service you selected earlier. And, we can take care of all the minute details- once you return home.

"Now, Kevin, I know this is all news to you regarding the Alaskan assignment, and I'll not interfere with any plans that you and Julie agree on. But, I'd like to help any way that I can. You're work and well-being are important. None the less, I don't wish for you two to be pressured on a time frame, or have a strain on your plans," Cecilia confessed, as she faced Kevin.

"Kevin, quickly said, "I think Julie and I will discuss this tomorrow during lunch, if she agrees.

"That sounds like a plan, Kevin. Maybe, at the Blitz Coffee Shop. Is that a good place for you at twelve noon tomorrow?"

"Sure, Julie, I'll plan to see you then. He started to exit the door, and Julie walked him to the foyer where they said their good-nights. Kevin looked somewhat puzzled. "We'll work this out, dear," he said as he departed without another word.

◄━

The next day during lunch Julie mentioned her dilemma at the Herald. "Kevin, I told Surich that I would try to go on the Alaskan trip, if- she was unable to make it. She has other issues preventing her from being in Alaska. It's not good timing, but do you think we could work together to get most of our plans for the wedding, and housing taken care of prior to my departure?"

"I'm just disappointed, Julie. I had hoped we could get plans underway, especially our housing, before I started to work. I'm just home from the service, and I really need your help since I've been away several months."

"I realize your situation, Kevin, but Surich is willing to help with our housing. We have two houses and one condo to view tomorrow. We may get some good ideas, quickly. If we can't agree on a house soon, you could live in my apartment a few weeks until we locate the best housing available. Mom is volunteering to narrow all items on our list, by helping with wedding plans," Julie offered. "And, we've already discussed most of these.:"

We'll see, we can discuss the options more after we look over some property tomorrow."

"Good, I'll see you at 2:00pm tomorrow with Surich. We'll meet at the Blitz after checking out the houses, okay?"

Over coffee at the Blitz the next day, Kevin was quiet and humorless. Twisting his lips, he kept shifting his weight, as he offered Julie more French vanilla creamer.

"Kevin, I know you're as upset as I am about my pending out-of-state travel, and my leaving at this inopportune time. But, I don't seem to have other options, since Surich can't commit to the Herald assignment. I surely don't intend to make this a habit. The team really needs my help. I have some contacts among the tribes that other team members do not possess. I may be able to get information about the cruise liner, if I can reach my contacts. I have affiliated with them on one other occasion, when there was a plane crash in the Yukon region." Julie mentioned.

Kevin was reconsidering plans, when Jay Falk walked in.

CHAPTER
EIGHTEEN

"**G**ood to see you two, Julie and Kevin. I see you love the atmosphere here too. This is one of my favored early morning stops. And, I really needed to speak with you, Kevin."

Kevin's eyebrows raised and crinkled, as he rose to grasp Jay's hand. "Have a seat, Jay, we're still enjoying our lattes. Care to have a mug?"

"Thanks, but I'll just have coffee." He motioned for the waitress. My time is somewhat short, as I have a meeting soon with the Herald team. Julie, you coming on into the office, I assume?"

"I should be there in a few minutes, but I needed this steaming cup of latte to brighten my day." She grinned as Jay agreed it was a plus.

Kevin, I'll get right to the point. Our group at the Herald really needs Julie's experience and help with the Alaskan assignment. Julie has mentioned that you two have many plans to consider, but we're including more security with our team this go-around. Julie's safety should not be compromised. We're preparing for risks, and will have a guide in Alaska to assist us; he is adept to the dangers in the territory, and very qualified to escort us to our destination."

"Jay, I know you are a capable investigator. Julie has been forthcoming with your skills, and devotion to the team. But, are you prepared for weather variables, and the ravages of the Alaskan wilderness?"

"That's why we are securing a guide, and other able-bodied men to assist us with elemental factors, and the territory. We know where the cruise liner was last sighted. We just need to confront other individuals who can help us with the information we need, and Julie has contacts from her previous trips into the area. She could be a great help."

"Jay, I know you've been a stand-by when Julie's had other dangerous assignments. If she goes, I want you to assure me, that you'll be close by at all times with a team approach. We are willing to delay our marriage for a short while, but I want to ensure her safety. We plan to proceed with our vows as soon as she returns and we can get our wedding plans and housing completed." Kevin's stern expression and commanding tone spoke volumes to Julie.

Julie just listened, amazed at Kevin's concern for her. And, if she had doubts about his convictions and love for her before, they had faded upon hearing his determinations for her.

"I know, Kevin. And, I wish to assure both of you that I'll do all in my power to promote safety and completion of our news gathering in a timely manner. Getting the cruise liner safely rescued, with the crew and passengers back to the United States, is our goal," he exclaimed.

When Jay departed the Blitz Coffee Shop, Kevin reassured Julie. "I feel more confident about your trip now, Julie. Let's just try to complete most of our wedding and housing plans before you leave Topeka."

◄━━

When Kevin and Julie met with Surich the next day, she was prompt to show them the housing and nearby neighborhoods that her realtor had shared with her. After they met the realtor near the locations, she showed them some great houses, locations, and rental condominiums that she had lined up for them. The prices were also reasonable. They were definitely impressed.

After a few hours of reviewing and discussing their options, Kevin and Julie chose the condo closest to Kevin's future employment, and to their parents. They were filled with joy over their rental agreement.

"Kevin, if we can get our belongings packed-up, you can get the movers to start the moving process while I work with Mom on our wedding plans."

One week later Julie had most of the wedding plans in order, and the movers were moving their furniture from her apartment and Kevin's home into the condo they were renting. Julie planned to stay with her mom when she returned from Alaska, until after their wedding.

◄━━

"Julie, I'm more comfortable with our progress and living arrangements now that we've mastered some of our plans."

"Yes, as I've prepared to leave this week-end, I can see a light at the end of the tunnel." Arriving at the airport, Kevin watched others boarding the plane and knew Julie was in good hands with a safe and caring team: the Herald News team with a guide and capable cohorts. Lingering at the gate, embracing and kissing each other good-bye, the couple stopped when the team uniformly called, "Julie, it's time to go!" Grinning, she departed his arms, and escaped into the plane.

Kevin watched as the plane taxied, and then soared from his sight. As moisture filled his eyes, he silently whispered, "Off on a daring mission," and began to pray,

> "Lord, watch over and protect the one of my heart. Bring her back safely to me, and help the group with their search. May their mission be fulfilled with help to those in need, and mercy for the Herald team. Amen."

Having finished his prayer, Kevin departed for home with more solace and peace from the Father of hope and light.

CHAPTER
NINETEEN

Two days after arriving in Alaska, Jay, Julie, and some of the Herald investigative team were able to locate some of Julie's friends near the Skagway area. The other members of the team were doing research via phone and community news of any possible leads of the missing liner.

Getting some possible sightings of the cruise liner from her friend, Mino, of the inhabitants near their hotel, Jay and Julie's team were encouraged. Mino suggested they fly by helicopter to search for the ship. If they could spot it again, they could radio for help to escort the liner to a safe port where all the occupants could be rescued.

The next day the search team set out with Mino and their guide to survey the area near the sightings. After being in flight almost five hours, Mino directed them to a remote area of the sea where the ice accumulations were hindering almost all ships nearby. Flying close to the forest near the frozen zone, they were able to spot a vessel barely moving.

As Mino and group flew nearby, the team saw white flags, and a few people were waving from the deck of the ship. As they hovered over the ship, they could hear shouts of.. help, help, help." The helicopter pilot was able to get a message down to the Captain that he would call for help for the crew, passengers, and vessel.

The team noted Princess Cruise on the side of the vessel: the missing liner. Ice was almost surrounding the ship. The pilot doing the search quickly radioed ahead to the nearest port authority their location, and that the vessel would need help with ice cutters, and/or airlift teams to assist with a rescue effort.

As the Herald team flew back to their base housing, they were thrilled to know that a rescue mission would now be sent to the cruise liner. They could call in a report now to the Herald. Julie would probably be able to return back to Topeka with her team soon.

Upon arriving back near Skagway, Julie immediately called Kevin to inform him of their sighting of the cruise liner. And, that rescue efforts were about to be underway. She knew that she would sleep well tonight, and so would all her team members.

"Glory be," she exclaimed, God does indeed work in mysterious ways, and our prayers are being answered. I shall be flying back into Kevin's arms as soon as our report is completed." She voiced to her friends.

Jay was exceedingly quiet as she approached him at the dining area that evening. "Do you still have concern about the rescue effort, Jay?" Julie voiced concern.

"I just hope the rescue efforts are possible with all the ice surrounding the Princess. Did the pilot get a verbal confirmation from the Coast Guard regarding a speedy rescue?"

"Jay, I didn't hear all of the conversation between the pilot and the captain. But, they should not have dismissed us if they had qualms about the rescue attempt. I'll call again this p.m. and determine if things are progressing as planned."

"Absolutely, Julie, let me know how things are moving. Let's keep our faith and hopes high. It will not be an easy task to get all the equipment and personnel flown into the area with success and expediency," Jay soberly hung his head with concern and empathy for those trapped in the ship with help needed.

As the Herald team waited patiently the next day, phone service was slow in coming. Julie was unable to reach the rescue team that evening, she tried again the next day.

Reaching Lieutenant Peterson of the airlift brigade, she discovered he was already in a rescue mode, but not of the Princess. His helicopter was rescue efforts in another area of a glacier. He reported there were two more missions he must see to before the Princess would be attended. He said he was trying to get other ports of call to assist with airlifts, but thus far all were involved with other rescues. The weather is just wreaking havoc with our rescues," Peterson confided.

Julie was able to contact Mino after several attempts. If he could assist, lives may be spared aboard the Princess. She pleaded, "Mino expedite all rescue efforts: supplies and food are needed for the crew and all passengers aboard the ship. Lieutenant Peterson confirmed some of the passengers are ill, and famished."

The next morning Mino was able to acquire another large helicopter to assist with airlift efforts. The first airlift was of a senior couple who reported of heroic efforts among the passengers to help sustain one another. Their food supply was dwindling, and there were other illnesses reported from the cruise liner.

As other passengers were rescued with some crew members, they reported that.. "yes, the vessel was seaworthy, but the captain did not anticipate the drastic weather changes. He had extra supplies aboard the ship, but they were pushing their capacity with extra passengers aboard," Mino confessed.

What a story Jay's group discovered of this lovely lady who ate little, and shared her food with others, consoled fellow passengers, and was able to prevent a suicide attempt. Just getting water had been an effort, a weakened passenger contributed.

"Help has arrived, be it a slow process. It could take weeks to get the Cruise liner back to port. But we're getting the passengers and crew airlifted as timely as possible," Mino solemnly reported.

"Julie, you need to get home soon. I'm not getting much done on our furniture arrangements, and this eating out daily is a challenge. I miss your touch and care the most, but I'm not much at keeping up the condo and my flights," he groaned. The location is great for convenience to work, home and places of interest, but not best without you, Julie."

"Kevin, I'll be home just as soon as things settle and we see the rescue is complete for the Princess passengers and crew."

Mino, our helicopter pilot, reports that he should have all personnel .and passengers rescued in another day or two. I should be able to depart with the Herald team then. How is your new job going?"

"I thoroughly enjoy the pilot position with American Airlines, and things are coming together. I need you home to finish our wedding plans as soon as you get the go-ahead to leave. I miss you, honey." She could hear him choke-up to speak.

Confirming her love for Kevin, Julie stated, "we should be home very soon." She silenced the phone as tears filled her eyes.

◄◄

As the Herald team gathered for dinner that evening at the Fastest Grill, Jay surprised Julie by mentioning Surich, her co-worker. "Julie, what do you know about Surich Placusky?"

"Why do you ask, Jay?"

"There was this guy by the hotel yesterday inquiring if she was with our group. He said she was a friend of his, and that he needed to contact her."

"Jay, she is a great reporter and friend."

"I didn't reveal any details of her whereabouts, but he seemed intent upon finding her."

"Jay, that info will not come from us. We'll not

give him anything regarding her whereabouts until I speak with Surich."

Back at the hotel, Julie promptly called Surich. Speaking of the successful mission, she gave a heads-up report of all accomplishments, and of the their plans to return home soon.

"Yes, we're anxious to get home especially with the weather outlook being colder than we're accustomed to in the States. By the way, there was a gentleman at our hotel inquiring about your whereabouts. He stated to Jay that he was a friend of yours."

"Oh heavens, Julie, be sure and don't mention where I live. He must be Alex Coscoff, the guy that has pestered me about returning to Alaska. I definitely don't wish him near me. He's caused me much pain. Please don't allow him to weaken your defenses and pry information. If he persists, I'll have to notify the Sheriff or secure some protection for myself. He doesn't have good intentions."

"We'll be careful to avoid him, Surich. Don't worry Jay has experience with security measures. Keep you chin up, we should be home soon."

The next day Julie briefed Jay about contacting Surich. He assured her that he would use security measures to prevent Alex from acquiring information regarding their team's departure. Fortunately, they were scheduled to leave Saturday.

Calling Kevin and her mom the next day, she grinned as she listened to their accolades upon hearing of their flight home Saturday.

"Julie, I'm sure I'll be back from my flight to London by the time your flight arrives in Topeka. Keep me posted on your whereabouts tomorrow. I must be at the airport to welcome you home. Your mom has helped me so much. I can't thank her enough. We'll get preparations for our wedding finished soon. Cecilia has many plans underway," he chattered nonstop with enthusiasm.

Saturday couldn't come soon enough for Julie. Having said her goodbye on the phone, she knew packing was her next chore. She had assured Kevin she'd request more time off from work when she returned home.

As the Herald team was packing their luggage, Jay stopped by Julie's room to relay that he had security in place to detect any sightings of Alex Coscoff. And, that he had not been spotted anywhere near their plane's airport.

"I have consolation just knowing he is not taking leave with us, nor is he near our flight area." Julie exclaimed to Jay.

"If he so much as appears near the airport in Topeka, Kansas, I've informed the security there to detain him until Chief Jarod gets an update from Alaska on his past activities, or criminal record. Julie, I'll protect you and Surich, as well as, anyone of our Herald group exposed to untoward activities."

As the plane departed for Topeka, team spirits were high.

CHAPTER
TWENTY

Arriving late Saturday night in Topeka, Kansas, Julie located Kevin and her mom at the airport almost as soon as she departed the plane. Rushing to meet them, she embraced Kevin. "I've never been happier to see you two." Her mom quickly reached out to her with tears of joy as she hugged her and kissed her forehead.

Kevin was slow to release his grip around her waist, but hurried to assist her with luggage. "I can't wait to see you safely home. And, congratulations on succeeding in your search and rescue attempts of the Princess. Is the team safe, and were all the passengers finally accommodated with shelter, food, and news to their loved ones?" Kevin kept questions coming as Julie tried to gather her luggage, slow her tripping heartbeat, and cease the trembling of her hands.

"Wow, what an endeavor, Julie. You can fill us in on all the trials and harrowing escapes for the passengers and crew of the ocean liner when you get home. I'm following you and Kevin to your condo; we have a dinner planned for you, Cecilia cried. Julie bade the Herald team goodbye as Kevin thanked all for the great accomplishments of the group. Julie assured Jay and the team that she would see them Monday with her reports from the mission. Kevin hurriedly escorted her to his vehicle and on to their home.

As they arrived and entered the condo, welcome signs were hanging from the ceilings with balloons and rainbow colored decor through-out the kitchen. "I'm astounded that you guys could get dinner, and the welcome you've given me. My heart is pumping with vigor, and my gratitude is pouring-out to you two for all your efforts to make this homecoming special. Mom and Kevin, thanks! I love you both," came from Julie's lips as she kissed Kevin, and then embraced her mom.

"Julie, I'm so happy you're safely home. You wouldn't believe all that you mom and I have complete with the condo and wedding plans," Kevin voiced as they unloaded Julie's luggage and hurried to the savor the food from the dining room.

"Enjoying the Chinese cuisine delectable, Julie lavished Kevin and mom with praise for their updating the condo, and completing most of their wedding plans.

"We'll get most everything in place soon for the wedding. Has Dad gotten his approval for his leave from the service," Julie inquired.

"Actually, he should arrive home any day now." Her mom was quick to respond with a huge smile. "He should have some welcomed time off: maybe several days. We may be able to take a little trip ourselves after the wedding, I'm hoping.

◄◄

Two weeks later the wedding was truly underway. Both Julie and Kevin were amazed how Cecilia had helped to make things come together. Julie's dress was exquisite, trimmed in delicate Chantilly lace and sequins which gave an exuberant glow to her creamy complexion, as complemented with the off shoulder bodice.

Kevin was obviously enthralled, as was Julie's dad with his lovely daughter; Mr. Peterson, who had obtained an extended leave from his work, was more than happy to do the honors of escorting Julie down the aisle. The couple radiated adoration for each other. Surich was Julie's matron of honor, while Jay was happy to serve as Kevin's best man.

As Kevin stood awaiting Julie's walk down the aisle, he captured her attention in his black tuxedo with his precision styled crew-cut blond hair, and dazzling blue eyes focused on none other than his soon-to-be bride.

The overtures from the ethereal-sounding music could almost melt the already warmed hearts of those attending. Then, the pre-planned wedding vows captivated the audience; one could hear the whispered awes from the gathering.

After the vows, came the reception set-up for the most impressive couple in town. The warm congratulations and well wishes were followed by waves of goodbye from the couple as they were off to the Cayman Islands for their honey-moon.

Both Cecilia and Jacqueline Seals were tearful to see their loved ones departing. But, Kevin and Julie just bubbled with joy as they embraced, then drove away for their long awaited destination.

TWENTY-ONE

"Wait a minute! If you think I'm going back to Alaska with you, you have another thought coming. Alex, I've had enough of your shady dealings while I was in Alaska. I have no intentions of getting involved with you again. Why did you make this trip to the States just to coerce me again? I made it clear to you before that I am finished with you!"

"Surich, you must realize that you and I were an item with our relations and business dealings in Skagway. If you hadn't balked on me, we could have had enough dealings for a well-planned life style. Surich, you were a smooth operator with your knowledge of the comings and goings of the Russian connection. Don't say you didn't enjoy some of the fringe benefits (like that cruise we made last year)," Alex kept smiling his cunning smile.

"You know that I had no idea at that time what you were up to. I'm not sure you really know the detriment that the Russian mob is contributing to our demise in the States. But I'll have no part in it. I was unknowing of your illicit deals to begin with, but I became wise, and I'll not follow suit with your plans again. I have friends here now. And my work is very promising at the Herald."

"How did you find me? Give me a break, and just leave. I'll keep quiet, if you'll leave me out of this."

"You're needed, Surich, especially with your contacts here. You can be a great benefit to my operation in Alaska. You're coming with me!" He stated, grabbing her arm.

Surich began crying as Alex reached her. "If you'll just leave and let me sort this out, we might could reach an agreement. Perhaps I could get a short leave of absence, or short vacation from work here to tie up some loose ends in Alaska with you. Then, you could go about your endeavors with another partner. I would like to get back to work here, and continue my career. Please give me some consideration, Alex."

"Okay, I'll go. I'm trusting your word, but don't try any capers, or you could end up in Alaska even sooner."

"Before he could reach the door, Surich cautioned, "you know some of your cohorts have been detained by the police, and you could be next." She stopped, regretting the words she'd spoken, when she saw his face aflame and anger mounting.

Alex turned on his heels. "Don't make any threats to me, lady. You know you're involved in this as much as I am." :"I've worked hard at my position," at the Herald. I will not enjoy relinquishing any success that I have enjoyed. I'm tired of fighting you. And, I think we can resolve our differences, if you'll cease your demands. I'm sure you can recruit others to take my place and accomplish your purposes."

"Let's just cover one base at a time. You're not just a partner, we have a relationship, Surich, or have you forgotten so soon."

Surich just lowered her head as tears continued to fall. Alex started for the door again with another warning. "I'll see you in the early a.m. Be ready and packed for our return to Skagway. I have immediate plans for our activities."

As he left, Surich hurriedly dialed Julie's number. *She should have returned from her honeymoon by now*. When Julie answered the call, Surich began to pour out her heart about Alex's threats. "I need help now, Julie!

"I'll do everything possible to thwart Alex's plans. I'll call Jay immediately, Surich, so he can halt your departure with Alex." Julie spoke gently to reassure Surich. "Especially, since the dude is threatening to report false charges against you to the Alaskan authorities, I'll make Jay aware of the urgence."

Trying to reassure Surich was not an easy task, Julie soon learned, as she told her of his connections with the police authorities here. "He'll start proceedings immediately to get you the help you need." Silencing the phone, she dialed Jay's number. Frantically, she explained Surich's worry and turmoil to Jay.

"Julie, I'll have a friend of mine sent to Surich's home now to get her to a secure location until we can get Alex into custody. We'll notify the Alaskan authorities of his activities here in the States. I'm of the opinion that the police in Skagway can give us some data on his background that could help us to detain him 'til we can get him back to Alaska. I'm almost positive we'll get him moving with the background check, and Surich's charges against him. Perhaps Surich will give us more evidence of Alex's illicit activities in Alaska."

"Thanks, Jay, Keep me informed."

"What's going on, Julie? I'm concerned about Surich, Kevin called from the kitchen. "Tell me, did Jay have more information? Is Surich a Christian? We need to have prayer for her tonight, and daily."

"I've never heard her mention any thoughts regarding God. But, we shall visit her and witness to her to support her as we can, Kevin. She is a great employee at the Herald and loves her work here."

Calling Surich back, Julie informed her that Jay was to get a security officer to her place and transport her to a safe location. "Surich, it may be to my mom's place. Be ready when the guy comes by. You'll be in good company at my mom's."

Surich hurriedly packed some clothes and personal items. She began to feel her heart rate slow, and muscles relax to know she now had a plan of safety. Waiting for her escort to Cecilia's, she remembered many of the past events in Alaska, and how Alex Coscoff had affected her job there. He had stressed her parents so with his escapades with the Russians, that they had moved to the coastal town of Sitka to gain some distance from his frequent visits.

After Surich's parents moved, she immediately sought a job in the States. And, with her parent's help she was able to escape from her troubled relationship with the crude domineering Alex. Her parents would've chosen to leave also had she not had two younger sisters in school near Sitka: they wished to finish the school term there.

Hearing a knock at the door, Surich peered thru the small window to see a guy she presumed was her escort to Julie's mom's. She carefully opened the door after establishing his identlty. Realizing her option to safety, she was ready- set to leave. "Eddie, I'm ready to head-out to Mrs. Peterson's house."

"Yes, I prepared to get you to safety and protect you, Ms. Surich. I've been friends with Jay for some time. Let's move."

As Surich and Eddie arrived at Cecilia's home, Julie and Jay welcomed them; Julie embracing Surich with-"we'll help you get this guy out of your hair," while Jay grasped Eddie's hand in greeting. Surich's eyelids were red and swollen with evidence of her recent tears as she followed Julie into the kitchen. Cecilia met her with a warm smile. Offering chairs and mugs of coffee as she took Surich's hand.

"I've been expecting you all. Surich, Julie has mentioned your unpleasant experience. I'm so sorry to hear of the ordeal. You're very welcome to stay with me as needed. I'll take your belongings to the room I have planned for you, as soon as we finish here. I have sandwiches and other snacks for you all. Julie promptly served the food while Cecilia whisked the luggage to the bedroom.

After Surich was settled in comfortably, and sipping on the latte that Julie had graced her with, Jay and Eddie joined them for food and drinks.

As the conversation lagged, Surich revealed to Jay how dire her circumstances were. "Jay, I have got to get out of Alex's grasp, or I'll lose my position at the Herald, and my security here in the States. I need your help."

"My security detail shall protect you with the vigilance they would their own mother. Just hang close to them until we get Mr. Coscoff bound for Alaska. Call ahead to work, and don't move out until we give the go-ahead. I suggest you avoid work tomorrow. Chief Jarod and I are planning to detain Alex Coscoff until we get evidence from Alaska to get him quickly transported with security to Skagway. When we capture him, we'll need you to sign a warrant for his arrest."

I'll gladly comply, Jay. I don't have another choice, if I'm to have any peace."

"Eddie will be here to secure the house, and the police personnel shall be assisting with your security as needed. Please keep your chin up, Surich, we'll get Coscoff," Jay's stern tone gave her hope as he and Julie departed.

◄━━

Kevin quickly embraced Julie when she returned home from her mom's. Rubbing his head, and seating her in the living room, he cautiously spoke. Honey, I heard from Commander O'Neal in Puerto Rico tonight. He is enticing me to return to Puerto Rico to give a briefing to new recruits at the Aguadilla Air Base."

"O'no, Kevin. Whatever for? Haven't you done your

full duty to the Air Force and America! I can't believe they would ask you to return so early after you've returned home."

"Julie, it would give the new arrivals an idea of what can go wrong on flights when on mission. I'm willing to go and help any way that I can to prevent sudden mishaps like I have incurred along the way. Although I'm out of the service, I have a lecturing circuit that I can attend to as a civilian at any given time. Julie this is a way to offer other services to my country." He furrowed his brow at her concern.

"Kevin, you are too kind to think of others after your ordeals. But, if you're willing, what can I say? I know you wish all recruits could avoid dire situations, and prevent catastrophes. But, please don't allow the Commander to extend your stay."

"Julie, it is only a one-time trip, and I really wish to do this. You can come along if you wish. I'll need to get permission from my flight director to be off a few days. Will you accompany me, or can you get off a few days?"

No, honey, I've been away too much already. I'll just stay in touch, and be close by if Mom or Surich need me. I'll also be in prayer for your travel."

"O' Julie, you know I love you very much and had rather be here altogether." As he held her and stroked her luscious brown hair, he was finding it difficult to think of leaving. They stayed embraced until the phone rang. Julie grasped the phone, thinking of Surich.

"Kevin, it's Alex," she whispered.

Ms. Julie, Surich is not answering her phone. Do

you know if she is home? She is usually not sleeping this early." Alex almost shouted.

"I think she is Alex. I spoke with her early this evening when she called and she said she was exhausted. I told her to get some rest."

"She had better hope that is all she's doing; we have a busy day tomorrow."

"I'll safely bet she is sleeping. She seemed tired when we spoke."

"If you hear from her, have her call me; it's urgent," he commented before the line silenced.

"Kevin I don't know how he got my number unless he saw it at Surich's apartment. I'm not staying here until he's gone!' I'm going back to my mom's when you leave out tomorrow."

The next morning Julie and Kevin left their condo at the same time. Julie to her moms, and then to work, while Kevin was off for his flight to Puerto Rico. He was still on the phone to Julie as he was boarding his plane. "Julie let's stay in prayer that Surich will get through this situation."

"You bet, Kevin."

"Stay safe, and no heroic actions, Julie. I'll be back soon," he spoke gently as he bade her goodbye; then silence.

◄━━

Surich slept very little and was wide-eyed when Julie arrived at her mom's. Julie did not mention that Alex had called her last night. I don't need to alarm her further, she contemplated.

"Good to see you up and about, Surich. I'm going

on into work. We have two assignments that's keeping us busy, but I'll stay in touch with you. Stay close to Mom today and don't venture out."

"O', you need not worry, I'm not stepping out of this area, I'm very comfortable here, and your mom is great company.

Cecilia was up and about getting breakfast for the three of them, including the security officer. She led them in prayer for everyone's safety, and a peaceful resolution to Surich's issues. They enjoyed a breakfast of ham croissants, fruit parfaits, and oatmeal.

"The food is splendid Mrs. Peterson, Surich exclaimed. I may never wish to leave your home."

"Thanks, Surich. I'm happy to have company, and to enjoy the friendship that I've embraced. I know this is a trying time for you; Julie, Kevin, Jay, and I'll be a support to you, as you allow. We also have a church nearby that I hope you'll acquaint yourself with. You're definitely invited to attend with some of us soon."

I'll look forward to a visit with you or Julie, I'm sure.

◄━

As Julie hurried along to work, she tensed with concern for Surich, and her mom's safety. She remembered her last encounter with the Russians when they were trying to gain information regarding the Witherton Files. She flinched as she recalled the shots fired at Finley as he attempted a break-in at her mom's. She reached for her cell phone and dialed Jay's number.

"Jay, I'm fearful of Surich's and Mom's safety since Alex is searching for Ms. Placusky today." She spoke by cell phone.

"What's happened, Julie? Has Alex been calling her again?"

"No, no. But, he's pestered me; and, I'm sure if he can locate Surich, he'll try to get her on a plane to Alaska."

"Julie, I'll beef-up security at your mom's until Alex is off to Alaska, and out of Surich's hair."

"Thanks, Jay, you've saved the day for me. I didn't sleep well last night worrying about this crisis. And, with Kevin out of town... I don't wish to have chaos for any of us again."

"Understood. He don't realize our capabilities in Kansas. Chief Jarod may have more news today that will help us get him into custody."

Jay and Jarod worked diligently to get the info from Alaska to pursue Alex's capture. By 2:00p.m, they had gathered enough evidence from the Alaskan authorities, and from Surich to arrest him. Once they located him- he should be at one of the local hotels they decided. After scanning several of the hotels in the area, they located his niche just north of Surich's home.

They approached his room and knocked on his door. Jarod and Jay could hear movement inside the room. "He must still be in his room, but sure is slow to answer our knock," Jay murmured.

Finally. The resident called out, "Who's there?"

Chief Jarod stated, "It's Jarod, I just need to

speak to you regarding a complaint of noise in the building."

Alex finally opened the door, and when he saw the police officer, he started toward the window. Jarod and Jay quickly subdued him. And, after positively identifying him, they escorted him to the police station. Reading him his rights took little time. They interrogated him, and promised Alex that he would be on a flight to Skagway as soon as tickets, and a flight could be booked.

Later in the day, Jay called Surich and Julie and informed them of the good news of Alex's capture, and their plans to expedite his flight to Alaska.

Surich sighed with relief at hearing the news. "Now, maybe I can have some rest and enjoy some peace again."

Jay mentioned, "since I'm off today from the Herald, I'll come by and enlighten you to the details surrounding Mr. Coscoff's capture, Surich."

"Yes, please, and enlighten me as to what steps I need to take to ensure my protection from the likes of him. And thanks to you and Chief Jared for all you've done."

"You bet, our pleasure, Surich."

When Jay arrived at Julie's moms the next day, it was Mrs. Peterson who answered the door. But, as they entered the kitchen area, Surich appeared shortly thereafter to confront Jay about the events leading to Alex's arrest. Cecilia excused herself.

"I'm appalled that Alex thinks I should bow at his beckon and call. He evidently thinks I'm a puppet that he can control with a string, and make demands of me. I'm definitely not interested now, or ever, with his endeavors. You wouldn't believe the threats I've experienced with him."

"Yes, Surich, I can imagine after I've met him and checked his police profile; he is way out of line for you. You seem too great a character for the likes of him. And, honestly, much too beautiful and elegant for his clandestine affairs." Are you a Christian, Surich? Julie and Kevin mentioned you in prayer these last few days. Are you involved in a church in this area?"

"Well, certainly, I believe in God, but I really have been more involved in my career since moving to Topeka. But, my family and I attended church in Alaska. We attended a Catholic church in Skagway. It was a wonderful community church, and we had friends there. I miss those good relations with my church..."

"I would love for you to attend the Catholic Church here with me next Sunday, if you'd like?"

"That would be great. I need to get back into church and worship again. I have missed that here." After Jay finished with the details of Alex's arrest, he tried to reassure that he'd stay in touch with the Alaskan authorities to help ensure her safety in the States.

"I shall see you Sunday for church services. Are you moving back to your place by then?"

"I should have all my things back by Saturday."

"Then, I'll arrive at your home by 10:00 am Sunday."

"Thanks, Jay, for everything, and I'll see you Sunday, Surich said, as Jay was exiting the house."

As Cecilia entered the foyer, she noted the flush

on Surich's face. "Surich, I'm happy you've met Jay, and he is a wonderful man; you can depend on his sincerity."

"I'm amazed that he has been so helpful and concerned for my safety. I can never repay the kindness you folks have shown me. Thanks for everything, and I should be moving out by Saturday, Cecilia."

Cecilia noted her eyes spoke volumes of how much she appreciated their care and help. "We'll be here for you whenever there's a need, Surich."

TWENTY-TWO

Kevin reached Aguadilla, Puerto Rico to meet Commander O'Neal who awaited his arrival late Tuesday evening in his office at Ramey Air Base. Kevin was quick to offer his salute. After saluting, the Commander greeted, "Good to see you, Kevin. Thanks for coming on such short notice. You had mentioned getting married when I last heard from you. Congratulation!"

"You bet, Colonel. I've never been happier. I'm just excited to get this briefing done, and get back to Julie, home, and now a new job awaiting me in Topeka."

After conversing about present events, Commander O'Neal was quick to give Kevin his assignment for the next day's briefing with the new recruits. "This is not a drill, just a casual seminar on how to deal with some crisis situations-you've encountered of late. We should be finished in two to three days, Kevin, once I get all the cadets together."

"That would be appreciated, Sir. Then, I can return to my work in Kansas. I'm hoping this Cuban Crisis shall be completely resolved by then. I wouldn't wish the new pilots to be faced with a situation of such magnitude this early in their careers."

"Nor would I, Kevin. I'm sure you remember all the tensions the U.S. experienced with Krushchev, and Fidel's brainstorming. Placing nukes in Cuba was just the final straw of our tolerance: to allow such a build-up in our backdoor. I'm thankful it was a concentrated effort of our nation to reach a peaceful compromise between the big powers and Cuba. God help us if we ever see such chaos again."

The classes went swiftly with Kevin engaging with the new recruits on various survival techniques he experienced while serving his country. He included his time in captivity with the Cubans and how he regained his freedom. There was good interaction with the cadets who appreciated his time and energy to help prepare them for unusual circumstances.

Upon arriving at his hotel that night, he was quick to call Julie to inform her that he would be arriving on the next flight on Wednesday evening.

"Oh, Kevin, I can hardly wait to tell you all the latest news. Surich is definitely doing better and back at her home. Now, maybe we can finish updating our Condo, and enjoying our time together. I'm learning to bake some delicious pies that Mom has been generous to pass on to me. Hurry home, and much love to you."

"And adoring love to you, Julie. I shall get home as soon as the airlines can deliver me," he chuckled.

The next day Julie was deep into work at the Herald when her phone dinged. It was Kevin. "Hello sweetheart, Julie greeted."Are you about to depart for home?"

"Yes, and I have met some wonderful recruits here

at the base. One guy, Patrick Finlay, is actually from Topeka. He has a few days off and will be traveling back with me on my flight to his home. I would like for you to meet him, Julie. Maybe we can stop by his place and meet his parents when he gets home."

"That sounds great. I shall expect you Wednesday. I'll be at the airport to meet you."

"By the way, Jay seems to be a great comfort to Surich. She states she's attending church services with all of us. Jay invited her. Maybe this will be a good experience for her to learn more about our worship, and meet new people. God works in mysterious ways. Let's continue to pray for her."

Julie had no sooner hung up the phone than it was ringing again. It was Phil Connor on the line.

"Julie, I need you to come to my office ASAP. There has been an accident aboard the Princess Cruise liner that is docked near Skagway. The Coast Guard is requesting our help again." Phil Connor, her boss, seemed breathless as he spoke. As Julie rushed up the stairs to his office, she kept hoping this would not be another event requiring a return to Alaska.

She had just entered his office when he reached out to greet her. "Julie, good to see you! I believe our team is needed again to pursue this bothersome follow-up story of the Princess liner. The rescue team was able to assist the Captain to get the liner docked near Skagway, but there was, then, an explosion aboard the ship. I don't know the details of damage or injuries involved, but I need you, Jay, and a few others, to book a flight there as soon as possible to gather the info for the Herald."

"Phil, does the government have any idea as to whether there might be a terrorist connection, or just carelessness?"

"Julie, good question, but that has not been mentioned. I can't imagine something of this magnitude on the vessel. I know the Herald team could probably unravel the cause as well as anyone. And, you'll give us a classic story as the reality of the causative factor unfolds, want you?"

"Well, anything seems possible as I think of the Russians having some close ties with the liners. Who knows their purpose, as we're ending the crisis involving Cuba and Russia. Do you think we can get our same team together to expedite a flight as early as tomorrow?" Julie questioned.

"Yes, I'll be contacting the other members right away and trying to book an early flight. Can you get Jay moving on this assignment, Julie? We shouldn't need many personnel, but you shall work with the Alaskan authorities to pinpoint the exact cause. "You'll be assisting with dispersal of the passengers, as well as, assisting with the investigation. The Coast Guard has already given their approval to your team, and would like any ideas about the passengers aboard the ship, including the crew."

"I'll get with Jay and start with preparations for the assignment, Phil. And, I'll also stay in touch. Kevin is due back in town Wednesday. I'll just have mom, or his parents to meet him at the airport."

As Julie called Kevin, she was trembling to think of his response. She prayed he would understand the urgency of the situation.

Kevin grabbed his cell phone on his way to lunch as it dinged. "Hello Julie, Is everything okay, or is Alex causing more chaos?"

"No, actually, Kevin, there has been an explosion on board the Princess Cruise liner while it was docked in Skagway. The Alaskan authorities are calling the Herald inquiring if we can assist them with their investigation, since we know some of the passengers and crew."

"O' Julie, I'm sorry to hear of this emergency. What can you all possibly know of these events, or passengers?" Kevin exclaimed.

"Well, we actually know very little, except- maybe comments from rescued passengers that we interviewed on our last trip. I know a couple of the men were very anxious to get on to Skagway. But, - don't know any significance to the present situation," Julie replied. Anyway, Mr. Connor wants us on the next flight to Alaska to assist the authorities with a duel-team Coast Guard investigation. And, of course, he is expecting a big story."

"Julie, I was hoping the other trip to Alaska was your last. Is it really necessary that you go again?"

"Yes, I'm afraid I am more qualified than most

with the surroundings, and the Princess Cruise Liner. I'll try to be back as soon as feasible. I don't like being away again. But, both you and I realize it's part of my job. Your mom or mine could meet you at the airport, Kevin. I love you so, and I should be home soon, and I'll stay in close touch.

"Okay, Julie. I'll pray for a safe trip, and good success. I'll miss you terribly," Kevin exclaimed.

Julie quickly called his mom and hers to confer with Jacqueline, and for one of them to meet Kevin at the airport.

When the Herald team arrived in Skagway, they were met by the coast guard personnel who were happy to get help to unravel this dire event. Fortunately, there weren't but ten injuries and two fatalities. As they gathered with the investigative team there was an on-going interrogation with four individuals and the Captain of the Princess liner. Both Julie and Jay recognized the captain's voice, as they had spoken with him many times when they had helped with rescue efforts on their last Alaskan assignment. He seemed stunned, to say the least about the explosion.

"I don't have any idea about what precipitated this explosion. We were docked and getting transportation arranged for the remaining passengers. These folks were still in a very weakened state. Having endured the long trip with scanty food and water supplies was bad enough. But, then to have an explosion to wreak havoc aboard was mind-boggling, to say the least," Captain Petrekov exclaimed.

As the Herald team listened to each individual's account, and activities, there was another investigation occurring in regard to the causative agent for this event.

Two days later, it was discovered by the forensic team that the explosion was caused by a default in the boiler room; that someone had used a secondary fuel that was not compatible with the new boiler system that was recently installed. There was only one person in charge of that duty, Eric Sayvinsky. Both Jay and Julie exchanged glances with Jay's eyebrows raised.

"Could he be a relative of Petroscoff Sayvinski who worked for the Herald in Topeka?" Julie murmured.

"Time will tell, Julie, when the search is completed." Jay commented. Obviously, he departed the vessel as soon as it docked," Jay volunteered.

The Coast Guard authorities had searched every cubicle of the cruise liner and had not found any trace of Eric. His room had been vacated, and all his belongings were gone.

Later that day, Julie and Jay obtained permission to search his last cubicle. As they scoured his room, Julie called out, "look, Jay, I recovered a newspaper from Skagway. Maybe he's en route there. See these two addresses circled in the housing ads, he must be headed that way."

Jay promptly notified the Coast Guard, and the phones began buzzing. That same evening the Skagway authorities notified the Coast Guard of the capture of a guy fitting Eric's description. Hopefully, the mystery would soon be solved of the person or persons involved in the explosion aboard the cruise liner.

The Herald team headed out to Skagway to pinpoint

any links between the Princess Cruise liner and Eric Sayvinski. If they could make the connection between the two brothers and their schemes to cause havoc to the American cruise liner, the authorities could start proceedings to capitalize on the capture of the villains. This case could soon be in perspective to begin prosecution of the criminals involved.

When the team arrived at the Alaskan authority headquarters, they were quick to learn that, yes, this was Petroscoff's big brother, and that there might be teamwork between the two. "Who could have guessed these two were related?"

Jay placed a call to Chief Jarod in Topeka. "Jarod, you need to notify the Alaskan authorities of Petroscoff Sayvinski's activities in the U.S."

He is the brother of Eric Sayvinski (a captured suspected bomber in Alaska). As Jay briefed Jarod on the Princess liner's explosion, and all events surrounding it, Jarod was quick to get his suspicions aroused. He started the wheels spinning to connect the dots to the brothers in question.

"We should be back into town tomorrow, and I'll meet you at your office to plan our next strategy," Jay confided.

◄━

Arriving at the airport in Topeka, Julie hurried to contact the Western Herald and convey much of the news gathered in Alaska. "Phil, I should have a complete report by early morning. I think you'll be surprised at the details we've gathered." Jay shall meet with Chief Jarod on some interesting developments, but I'll be in to give you an earful."

Connors chuckled, "I'll be interested to see the report and have you back with us, Julie. Be safe, see you soon."

As Julie departed the aircraft, she said her good-byes to the Herald team, and scouted the area for Kevin. She had just gathered her luggage, when she came face to face with her beloved husband. He quickly grabbed her about the waist in his embrace. He bent to kiss her as she encircled him in her arms, then, passionate kisses were a part of the blooming daylight hours. As they walked toward Kevin's parked vehicle, Julie murmured, "I can't wait to get home and realize how God has blessed us with a safe return again. Thanks be to God," she replied as they prepared to leave the airport.

"Julie, I'll be happy to try some more of your cooking, and the great pies that your mother has convinced me you've been baking." His sparkling blue eyes lit-up to reveal more than words could say. "But, I have plans for our dining out tonight, if you agree."

All Julie could do was squeeze Kevin's hand in reply, until her voice returned. She, then murmured, "I'm all for that, and, what else is in store for us?" She lifted her eyebrows

Kevin clasped her hand in his and quickly put the car in motion: the other hand on the wheel, as he replied, "I have great plans for tonight, never doubt what awaits our evening or our future." He smiled warmly and continued to keep her guessing...

THE END

THE END

EPILOGUE

Kevin and Julie are happily married and living in Topeka, Kansas. They are now parents to a one year old son, Sam Jr.: named after Kevin's father. Julie is expecting another child in eight months, hopefully a girl. She is still with the Western Herald and has advanced to editor of major news stories. She plans to work a few more weeks, then, maternity leave.

Kevin is still piloting his transcontinental flights near four days per week. He loves being home more with Sam Jr. who is growing more like his Dad every day. They could not be happier, as Sam is now saying-'Dad-da' with outstretched arms; a big smile spreads across Kevin's face. Sam is ready for his playtime with Dad, and Charlie, the new pup in the family.

The Seals new home is being constructed close to Kevin's mom and dad. His dad is now retired and Jacqueline feels more secure, especially, since she is dealing with heart disease. Their travels abroad are more convenient now that Kevin is to pilot many of their flights.

Julie is fortunate not to have any further contact with her previous kidnappers, and is enjoying the peace and safety of being home with Sam Jr. more often.

Kevin did interact with his former prison guard, Joe's, Aunt Cornelia, by way of the Catholic Church. And, Joe's wife received the funds, and help needed, for her impending surgery. Joe's Aunt Cornelia states she is forever grateful to Joe and his friend, Kevin Seals for their Christian faith, brother hood, and care for one another. She states she hopes for much better relations between Cuba and the U.S. now that the threats of war have been eliminated.

ACKNOWLEDGEMENTS

To- God, for his love, grace, and guidance in my life.

To- Jennifer, friend, prayer partner, encourager, mentor, and unfailing supporter, to get this novel in print.

To- Jerry, retired Sergeant in USAF for his expertise, contribution to military service, and to my writing of this book.

To- Larry, Megan, and Hannah for the love, and encouragement in my life's endeavors to serve others.

To- Max, a former Navy Seal, for his service to our country, and his kindly contribution in knowledge and photography.

Thanks and God's Blessings to each of you.

Printed in the United States
By Bookmasters